This is a work of fiction. Names, characters, places, and incidents either are the product of the author's imagination or are used fictitiously. Any resemblance to actual persons, living or dead, events, or locales is entirely coincidental.

Published by Laxsaro Publishing / September 2009

ISBN: 978-0-9825438-0-1

I would like to say a big thank you to the following people:

First and foremost to my soul mate, your unfailing love and support are beyond measure.

Andi and Mary Jo, who listened to my hare-brained ideas for stories, and still read the book.

To all of my beta-readers, your feedback and support was invaluable.

Jen, your library of books helped tremendously. And last but not least to Jocelyn, who may just show me her wings one day.

CHAPTER ONE

This is no ordinary fairy-tale but I shall start it just the same... Once upon a time, eleven years ago to be precise. In a land, oh, just around the corner, lived a young girl called Faedra. Her mother and father doted on her and at the tender age of just six years old she considered herself to be the luckiest little girl alive. That was until her world, suddenly and without warning, came crashing down around her...

University Hospital, Norwich, England.

Faedra sat in the cushioned hospital chair that was positioned in the hallway just outside the room her mother occupied. She could hear the voices inside the room behind the closed door. One of them she recognized. It was the voice of her father sounding much more anxious than usual, talking with growing concern to whom she assumed was the doctor. The other voice sounded like it was trying to remain calm, but she could sense that bewilderment was bubbling just below the surface.

Her father, Henry, had told her to sit outside for a moment while he talked to the doctor. She was trying hard to block out the voices by concentrating on her feet that were swinging nonchalantly below her, but try as she might she could still hear every word they said.

"There must be something you can do?" Henry pleaded.

"I'm so terribly sorry, Mr. Bennett, but we have never seen anything like this before," replied the doctor.

"Is there a cure?"

The doctor's voice rung heavily with disappointment." I wish I could tell you there was, but we have tried everything we know and her organs are still shutting down."

"Well, try something else!" Henry raised his voice in frustration. "I can't lose my wife, I just… can't." His voice cracked.

"Henry?" Faedra's mother, Lillith whispered.

"I woke you sweetheart, I'm sorry. What do you need?"

"Don't be angry with the doctors, Henry. It's not their fault."

"But there has to be something more they can do…" he broke off.

"Henry," she paused. "I need to see Faedra."

Faedra's head snapped to attention at the mention of her name and her feet grew still. She wanted to jump off the chair and run to her mother's side that instant, but knew that she should not have been listening to them in the first place. So she waited patiently until she was called. After what seemed like an eternity in Faedra's undeveloped mind, the door clicked open and her father stood in front of her and forced a smile.

She looked up at her father and examined his features. The kind brown eyes that she loved so much looked back at her in agony. She could read the pain on his face even though she knew he was trying so very hard to hide it from her. At that moment she realized, with much sadness, that her mother was not going to be with them for very much longer.

Her father was tall, standing before her, and he looked tired, exhausted in fact. His dark blonde hair looked unkempt, and his usually clean-shaven profile was half covered in a dark fuzzy overgrowth where he had not shaved for the last couple of days since her mother had unexpectedly fallen ill. He held out his hand for her.

"Mummy is asking for you, Princess."

Faedra took hold of her father's offered hand and slid herself down off the chair. His hand felt shaky, something she had not experienced whilst holding her daddy's hand before. It was always so strong, so sure. A sinking feeling grew in Faedra's stomach, and her heart started to quicken. She stuck closely to her father's side as he walked her into her mother's hospital room.

Lillith lay motionless in the big mechanical bed that was tilted up at the back enabling her to sit up. Faedra glanced at all the different kinds of monitors, wires, and tubes that were hooked up to her mother, and then focused on her mother's face to try and escape the fear those things were instilling in her. As she reached the bed Lillith held out her hand, and Faedra took it as her father simultaneously dropped the hand he was holding.

"Faedra, my darling girl," Lillith cooed. "Now you need to be strong for Mummy and Daddy, okay?"

"Okay, Mummy," Faedra whispered.

"I have something for you," she looked up at her husband. "Henry, could you please pass me that bag?" She pointed to a small gift bag sitting on the table across the room.

"Now, this is a very special gift and you must promise me that you will treasure it always," she told Faedra as she handed her the bag.

Faedra's little hands could not open the box inside the bag quick enough, but after a few moments, she had pulled the wrapper off, and lifted the gift from it's box with care. Her eyes grew wide with wonder as she stared at her present.

It was a figurine, standing about eight inches tall. A beautiful fairy was sitting atop a majestic black horse. The fairy had long red hair and silver wings flecked with emerald green that stretched proudly out behind her. She was wearing a blue skirt from which tiny bells hung. The horse was black as midnight and regal in stature with a long thick mane and tail adorned with silver stars.

"Oh, Mummy, she's so pretty. What is her name?"

"Her name is Arianne. I know how much you love horses and you know how much I love fairies so I thought this gift was perfect, it will always remind you of me. You'll keep her safe for me won't you?"

"I promise, Mummy. I will look after her always."

Lillith bent forward to kiss her daughter on the forehead. Tears welled up in her eyes, she looked up at her husband and mouthed for him to take Faedra away. At that moment Henry knew he was losing his wife, and he swallowed hard, biting back the tears that were searing behind his eyes as he took hold of his daughter's hand once more.

"Mummy needs to sleep now, Darling," Lillith whispered, knowing it would be the last time she saw her daughter.

"Okay, Mummy, I love you."

"I love you too, Darling. Forever and ever."

Court of the Light Fae, The Land of Azran

The Guardian strode with purpose through the magnificent double oak doors that led him into the Great Hall of the king who reigned over the Light Fae in the Land of Azran. The sword that hung from his waist swung with grace from side to side with the momentum of his footsteps. He ran a hand through his sleek blonde hair and looked around.

This hall never ceases to make me feel humble, he thought.

The ceiling towered many stories above him, held up on either side by imposing stone pillars. The pillars were intricately carved with the figures of various royalty and nobility that had ruled this land throughout the ages. Stained glass windows that stretched from half way up the walls to high above depicted many scenes of nature from several different realms, including The World of Men. The reason for those scenes was because the fae controlled nature. In fact, it was their responsibility to make sure that nature in all realms continued to thrive and to sustain the inhabitants within them.

His eyes were diverted to the floating chandeliers that lit the hall from above. The chandeliers followed the movements of whoever occupied the cavernous room, lighting the way for that person or persons wherever they should be within its walls. The candles flickering behind the crystals created dancing sparkles along the walls and the floor.

The Guardian smiled at the fae magic of the light that showered him from above and then brought his focus back to the unpleasant task at hand. He stepped up his pace for the remainder of the way down the long stone floor leading up to the throne where the king was seated.

The king, usually so stoic in his demeanor, sat fidgeting with his robes as he waited impatiently for The Guardian to reach him. Coming to a halt at the foot of the steps upon which the thrones sat, the Guardian got down on one knee and bowed his head.

"Is it true?" the king questioned abruptly.

"Yes, Your Majesty," the Guardian replied, rising when the king requested he do so with a gesture of his hand. He watched as the king's eyes filled with sadness.

"When?"

"Not more than one hour prior, Your Majesty."

"And the amulet?"

"Lillith passed the amulet to Faedra before she died, Your Majesty."

"The child is but six years of age," the king stated with concern.

The Guardian could see the king's face tense with worry and attempted to calm him.

"Sire, she is the next legitimate Custodian. Lillith hid it within the figurine of a fairy."

"Did she indeed?" the king smiled. "I did always admire her resourcefulness."

"Yes, Sire."

"Do you have any further information regarding why Lillith was on her way to see me when she was intercepted?"

The Guardian hung his head. He was assigned as Lillith's guardian, but she had sent him on an errand. The next thing he knew was that Redcaps had attacked her on her way to the portal, and he had reached her too late.

"No, Your Majesty. Nothing new has presented itself thus far."

"You know what you must do now." It was more of a statement than a question.

The Guardian's eyes shone with confusion as he looked at the king.

"But, Your Majesty, I have failed both you and Lillith."

"Guardian, you are young. This was your first assignment in the World of Men, and I paired you with Lillith because she had much to teach you, not the other way round. I have confidence that you have learned from this unfortunate turn of events and will not let it happen again. Make sure you do not fail little Faedra, she has much to learn, but it will be a while before we have to cross that bridge. Her mother should have been the one to teach her. That task, young Guardian, now lies in your hands. Do not let me down."

"No, Sire. Thank you, Sire." He bowed his head and the king nodded his acknowledgment.

The Bennett cottage, Spixworth, England

Faedra sat on the swing in the back garden, watching everyone coming and going from her vantage point. Friends and relatives she recognized, and others she didn't. It seemed like an endless stream to her. They were all dressed in similar clothing. Everyone wore black, and they looked like flies buzzing in and out of her home.

It was the afternoon, and her father was holding a wake for everyone who had attended the funeral earlier that day. She had watched in tears as her mother was buried that very morning at the local village church. Then the procession had made its way back to her house, and people had been milling about ever since. Some of them were crying. Others looked saddened. To Faedra the whole thing seemed like a blur. She couldn't quite understand why her mother wasn't coming back. Her father had told her she had gone up to heaven to be with the angels, but that didn't make sense to her either. Why would Mummy rather be in heaven with the angels instead of here with the people she loved?

She watched almost hypnotically as a well-meaning relative wandered over to where she was sitting on her swing. It was a warm summer's day and the sun shone in a cloudless blue sky. Birds were taking a bath in the little birdbath her mother had lovingly erected at some point in the past. She stared at the birds for a moment remembering all the times she had sat with her mother, and watched as they splashed around in the water. Her mother loved the birds. In fact, her mother loved all of nature, and had passed that love down to Faedra.

"Hi, Faedra," Uncle Leo announced as he approached the swing.

She turned her attention to him for a moment. Uncle Leo was her father's brother, and her favorite uncle. He didn't look that dissimilar from her father especially as they were both wearing a black suit that day, although he was a couple of years younger. He also had kind eyes, a warm hazel brown, and tousled dark blonde hair. He was not quite as tall as her father, but about the same build. He kneeled down in front of her and took hold of her hands.

"Hey, Uncle Leo," she said quietly.

"What are you doing out here all by yourself?"

"I'm watching the birds in Mummy's birdbath, see," she pointed towards the birds still splashing water over their backs with their wings. "They love Mummy's birdbath.

Mummy and I used to sit and watch the birds for ages." Her voice cracked as the truth was starting to sink in that she would never again sit with her mother to watch the birds.

"She's not ever coming back, is she?"

"No, Darling, I'm afraid she's not."

Big fat tears started to escape from Faedra's eyes and rolled down her cheeks to splash on her dress.

"Why not? Why does she want to be in heaven with the angels, doesn't Mummy know we love her more?"

Leo wrapped his arms around his little niece, using all his self-control to fight the tears that were welling up in his eyes also. He had loved Lillith like his very own sister, and was desperately sad to have lost her, too, but even more so to see the pain that his brother and niece were now suffering at their loss.

"It's not fair, Uncle Leo," Faedra cried. "I want her back."

"I know, Sweetheart, we all do but we have to be strong now."

Leo held onto his sobbing niece, smoothing her hair with his hand.

I would never have imagined in a million years how hard this moment would be, he thought.

He had no words to take Faedra's pain away. Nothing he could say would comfort the little girl he loved so much, so he just held her for several minutes and let her sob into his shoulder

"Leo," Henry called from the back door, "I need your help in here for a moment."

"I'll be there in a minute, Henry," Leo called back.

Leo pulled back from Faedra, gently loosening her grip, and looked into the reddened, tear soaked eyes of his little niece.

"Your daddy needs me, Faedra, I'll be back in just a minute okay."

"Okay," she sniffed. "Uncle Leo?"

"Yes."

"I love you."

"I love you too, darling."

Leo planted a kiss on her forehead and straightened himself up. Faedra watched as he turned and headed towards the house before she returned her attention to the birdbath once again. A moment passed, and the birdbath became blurry behind the tears that began to well up in her eyes and roll down her cheeks, and she wasn't sure at this point if she would ever be able to stop them. Something cold and wet touching her hand distracted her, it made her jump and she pulled her hand away sharply. She wiped the tears from her eyes with the heel of her hands so she could see with more clarity what she had just felt.

When Faedra looked down, two molten amber eyes greeted her, but this time their owner was not human. In fact, they belonged to a big white dog that was sitting in front of her. She looked around perplexed to see if she could see to whom the dog belonged. There was no one around other than the people in the house and she doubted that any of them would have brought a dog to a funeral.

Her home was a very old English country cottage located in heart of Norfolk. You had to drive down a tiny country lane, and then onto an even narrower long dirt driveway to get to it. It wasn't the type of place you went without a purpose. Fields on three sides, and a thick stand of trees at the back with a little stream meandering its way through it, surrounded the cottage. No wonder her mother loved it here. You couldn't be much closer to nature if you tried. Maybe the dog had come from the woods at the back, she was certain she hadn't seen him coming from any other direction, not that she had been paying that much attention.

"Hey, boy," she said, stroking the dog on the top of its head. "Where did you come from?"

The dog whimpered and laid his head on her knee, not once taking his eyes from hers. She was overcome by an overwhelming sense of comfort as she stared into its soft amber eyes. It was almost as if he could sense that she was in pain and wanted very much to take that pain away from her. Even as the thought entered her mind the dog sat upright again and licked the tears from her face. She responded by throwing her arms around him and burying her face in his soft white fur. She wasn't quite sure how long she had been hugging the dog until she heard a familiar voice.

"Faedra?"

She reluctantly pulled away from the dog and looked up into the worried eyes of her father.

"Yes, Daddy?"

Her father ran his hand through his hair and looked at his daughter. He was overwhelmed by how she looked like a miniature version of her mother. Every time he looked at her he could see Lillith. The same beautiful bright blue eyes with dark lashes that went on forever, and thick curly red hair that tumbled half way down her back. He felt blessed to have the two most beautiful women in his life. He missed Faedra's mother with an ache so fierce he thought his heart would shrivel up and die. But was thankful he still had his beautiful daughter and vowed to do his very best to keep her safe.

"Where did he come from?" he asked, looking at the great white dog standing next to his daughter in a way Henry could swear was protective.

"I don't know, Daddy. He just turned up, isn't he beautiful?"

"Yes, he certainly is. He looks like a Great White Pyrenees."

Henry checked his thoughts. Usually he would have been very unnerved seeing a dog the same size as his daughter in such a close proximity to her, but like Faedra all he felt was a sense of comfort.

"Can I keep him, Daddy?"

Henry's eyebrows shot up. He wasn't expecting that question.

"Well…" he paused.

"Please, Daddy."

Henry knew the moment he looked into his daughter's pleading eyes that he was defeated. He also knew the dog could not replace her mother, but if this dog could give her just one ounce of comfort then it would be a welcome addition to their family. Right at that moment, gazing deep into his little girl's eyes that were so full of pain, he would have given her anything to ease it.

"Okay, you can keep him."

"Oh thank you, Daddy! Do you hear that boy? You can stay with me."

Henry watched the dog wag its tail as Faedra threw her arms around him and again bury her face in his fur.

"What are you going to call him?" Henry asked.

"Faen," she declared without missing a beat. The dog's ear pricked up. He pulled away to look at her, and Faedra thought she saw the dog smile, if it were possible for dogs to smile. She didn't know, but she didn't linger on the thought, and wrapped her arms around the giant dog's neck once more.

"That's an unusual name."

"I know, but it suits him, doesn't it?" she said looking proud of herself.

"Whatever you say, darling. But if you keep him, then you are responsible for taking him for walks and cleaning up after him."

"I will, Daddy. I promise." She released Faen from her grip. "Come on, Faen, I'll show you my room. That's where you're going to sleep from now on."

Henry watched as Faedra lowered herself off the swing and wandered towards the house, followed closely by Faen wagging his enormous shaggy tail, and he scratched his head at the sight.

Present Day

Faedra pulled down the indicator lever on the steering wheel to signal she was turning left. The soft tick tick noise it made instilled a sense of relief in her as she turned onto the driveway that led to the cottage. She was home, and tomorrow was Saturday. She only made it half way down the driveway before her shaggy white dog came bounding up towards the car to greet her.

She stopped her car and beamed at him, rolling her window down as he placed his giant front paws on the car door and leaned his head in to plant a lolloping wet kiss on her cheek. She laughed as she grabbed a thick handful of fur on either side of his head, and leaned her cheek against the side of his face. This had become their daily ritual since Faedra had started driving and had gotten herself a job. She had taken a year off before she started college so she could get a job and save some money. College didn't come cheap these days. Her father had offered to pay, but she did not want him to shoulder all of the cost on his own.

"Hey, boy. Yes, I love you too," she responded to another sloppy kiss.

She leaned over to the back door, and pushed it open from the inside.

"In you get," she told him.

Faen wagged his tail voraciously and did as Faedra asked. She pulled the door closed and carried on down the driveway towards the cottage while Faen panted his hot breath in her ear. Upon turning a sharp bend in the driveway the cottage came into view. She never tired of its beauty, or the warm feeling it gave her just to look at it. The cottage was many hundreds of years old, and had been handed down through the family for generations. Her dad had completed many restorative projects on it since her mother had inherited it before Faedra was born. This in itself was a sad thing because that meant she had never known her grandparents. They had both died in a car accident before she was born. After living with the pain of loosing her own mother, Faedra felt full sympathy for what her mother must have gone through, losing both her parents in one fell swoop. Although, her mother had been much older than Faedra when it happened to her. She was already married to her father, Henry, and pregnant with Faedra.

The cottage had cream walls with an array of black oak beams that were exposed both on the outside, and on the inside. A beautiful climbing rose crept up the wall on a trellis and was in full bloom, exhibiting an abundance of bright sunny yellow petals. Her mother had planted it the year Faedra was born, and she had watched her father carefully tend the plant ever since.

Her father had also added a few more rooms on the back of the cottage, making it twice the size of the original dwelling. The living room, dining room, and two of the upstairs bedrooms were original and they were Faedra's favorite rooms. You almost had to duck when you walked into the living room the ceilings were so low. People had been much smaller in stature when the cottage was first built. But the living room was a complete contrast to the dining room that Faedra had lovingly named 'The Great Hall'.

The dining room was a cavernous room with an imposing brick fireplace at one end. A ceiling that towered two stories high was handsomely finished with exposed black oak beams running parallel to each other for the length of it. A staircase ran up one side of the room to a door at the top that led to her bedroom. She made sure she kept the front bedroom for herself, even after her father had finished a beautiful new room for her towards the back of the house. She had resisted, and with sensitivity, declined. There was something about the history in the old section of the house that she didn't want to be parted from.

Faedra pulled her car in beside her father's. He worked from home, had done ever since her mother died. For that she had felt blessed, that his job enabled him to stay at home so she had not had to be shipped off to a childcare provider every day. This turn of events had also made them very close. She loved her father with all her heart, and he felt the same about her. She smiled when she saw the other car parked next to her father's. It belonged to her uncle Leo. He had been an integral part of her upbringing, too, and she always enjoyed seeing him when he came round to visit.

She opened the door to let Faen out, and reached in to grab her bag that had been thrown precariously on the back seat when she had left work earlier. Faen waited by her side until she closed the door. He looked up at her and wagged his tail.

"Thank God that week is finished with," she told him. "I'm not sure I could've taken much more of Mr. Thompson. I honestly don't know why he's got it in for me."

Faen barked, as if agreeing with her.

"You know, boy, sometimes I could swear you understand every word I say."

She walked the few steps it took to reach the front door, kicked off her shoes inside the front porch, and lifted up the old-fashioned, black wrought iron latch on the door that led into the living room. The door would have initially been the exterior door and was the original from when the cottage was built. The porch was built much more recently in the cottage's history, probably by her grandparents.

The latch made its familiar chinking sound, a sound full of history and memories. It must have been lifted many thousands of times over its history, sometimes to welcome people in, and sometimes to bid them farewell, the memories it held seemingly endless. The quickening of a heartbeat when someone, patiently awaiting a loved one to return home, heard the latch chink. The relief, when an unwelcome or irritating visitor exited. Faedra's memories of walking through this door had always been happy ones except for one solitary entrance, the day her mother died, and she knew it would never welcome her mum home again. She let out a sigh.

As she swung the door open she felt the need to duck, even though the ceiling was at least a foot taller than she was. She looked around the cozy living room. There was a fireplace in here also; actually there was a fireplace in all the original rooms of the cottage as back in the day that was the only way to heat the house. She listened for signs of life and could hear voices coming from the kitchen.

"Come on, boy. They're in the kitchen."

She closed the living room door and wandered through another door to the contrastingly spacious dining room. The kitchen was located on the other side. Faen followed at her heels. He very rarely let her out of his sight when she was home.

"Hi, guys," she called as she reached the kitchen.

Her dad, uncle and her uncle's wife, Nicki, were all seated around the kitchen table, situated in the center of the room. They had their hands wrapped around cups of tea, and a plate of cookies sat in the center of the table. Faedra strode over to where her dad was sitting, and planted a kiss on his forehead then leaned past him to grab a cookie.

"Hey, Dad."

"Hello, Darling how was your day?"

"Oh you know, the usual."

"Mr. Thompson still treating you badly?"

"I don't know why you put up with his crap, Faedra," Uncle Leo chimed in, "I would have told him where to stick his job a long time ago."

"Thanks, Uncle Leo, but I need the money and it's not for much longer, I'll be starting college soon." Faedra made her way around the table to where her uncle sat, and leaned over to wrap her arms around his neck. "I'll survive, I promise." She smiled her cheeky grin at him and planted a kiss on his cheek.

"Well, you have the patience of a saint, that's all I can say," Leo continued.

"Hey, Nicki, what are you doing this weekend?" Faedra asked, quickly changing the subject of her dire working arrangements.

Her uncle had met Nicki not long after her mother had died, and Faedra had taken to her straight away. Although Nicki was a good ten years older than herself she had treated Faedra like a sister, and taken her under her wing. She was happy that her uncle had found such a wonderful person, and wished that her Dad would do the same. It had been nearly twelve years since that fateful day, and her Dad had never been interested in meeting anyone else even after all these years. She worried all the time that he would be so alone when eventually the inevitable happened, and she moved out.

"We are attempting to take your Dad out on the boat tomorrow, get him out of this house for a change," Nicki replied.

Faedra watched as her father raised his eyes heavenward. She knew her uncle had been trying to get him out to meet new people, mainly of the female variety, for a while now and sympathized with her dad after he had confided in her that he felt like a prize bull being paraded around a judging ring.

"That sounds like fun, Dad. I'd go with you if I didn't already have plans. I was going to invite Nicki to come with us to Strawberry Fair tomorrow."

"Thanks, Fae, but you're already taking Amy and Zoë, and Faen no doubt. It would have been just a little squashed in the back of your car."

She had a point, Faen let out a little whine.

"Don't worry, you're still coming," Faedra told him, and he wagged his tail.

Since he had turned up that day of the funeral they were virtually inseparable apart from when social decorum dictated. He could not go with her to school or to work, but waited patiently each day until she came home, and then didn't leave her side until the next morning.

"It's a good job Zoë loves you almost as much as I do," she told him kneeling down to rub his velvety soft ears. "You can ride in the back with her, she'll love that." She turned to her family. "Well, excuse me everyone, I'm going to get changed and run out to the barn. It's a beautiful evening for a ride."

"Hey, young lady," her dad called as she was headed in the direction of her bedroom. "You still haven't told me what you want to do for your eighteenth birthday it's just around the corner, or have you forgotten?" There was a hint of sarcasm in his tone.

Faedra raised her eyes at Faen, who was looking at her excitedly.

"Dad, I've already told you, I would like a small dinner here with you guys, Amy and Zoë, and I will be in seventh heaven. So don't go planning anything big for me will you, I don't want any fuss, promise?"

Her father let out a sigh, he would love to give his little girl a big birthday bash, but knew she wouldn't enjoy it, and had to be satisfied with a small, family and friends get together instead.

"Okay, darling, I promise." his voice was laced with disappointment.

CHAPTER TWO

Faedra sprinted up the stairs to her bedroom, followed as usual by her faithful friend. She drew up the latch on the door, which was also of the original old wrought iron variety, and entered her room. Throwing her bag clumsily on the bed, its contents fanned themselves out all over the comforter because the clasp was not closed securely enough. She gave the mess a look of nonchalance and shrugged her shoulders. It was the weekend and she didn't care, it could be tidied up later.

Her room was spacious, and located above the living room, but unlike the room below hers, this one had tall vaulted ceilings. Another fireplace stood on the same wall as the door, and she assumed it connected to the imposing fireplace in the dining room that was perpendicular below. The walls were painted in a muted yellow color and the windows were dressed with floral drapes that looked completely at home in the old cottage. On the opposite wall to the fireplace, and to the left of the window stood her dresser, with a beautiful antique vanity mirror, and an array of toiletries and cosmetics. The type that adorned most of the dressers owned by seventeen year old girls. On the other side of the window was a desk. It was more modern and looked very out of place in her quaint bedroom.

A beautiful heirloom doll's house stood on its own platform opposite her bed. Her mother had given it to her when she was a child, and had told her the story behind it. She had treasured it ever since. Her grandfather had built it with love for her grandmother, who had passed it onto her mother when she was a child. Her grandfather had also made all of the furniture inside the house, and she often stared in awe at the intricate detail of the tiny pieces, wondering how two big human hands could have created such delicate objects. There was an old wicker chair next to the doll's house with a fleecy pale green bathrobe draped over it.

On the wall next to the fireplace there was a small built-in closet that she had renovated, adding a glass door and shelving, to be a showcase for her spectacular collections of fairies. Her favorite, Arianne taking center stage. She had started collecting them ever since her mother had given her the beautiful figurine of a fairy on a stunning black horse, the day she died.

"You don't think I'm being mean, not letting Dad throw me a big birthday bash do you, boy?" she asked Faen as she opened the door to her collection, reached in and carefully picked up the figurine of Arianne. "But it's just too close to Mum's anniversary, and I can't bring myself to celebrate when it's that close."

Faedra had never felt compelled to celebrate her birthday at all, as it fell just a few days after the anniversary of her mother's death. Faen leaned up against her leg and let out a small whine. She admired the figurine for a moment with sadness. It was the most beautiful fairy she possessed, but it was linked to the saddest memory she possessed also.

"Ouch, here it goes again," she winced, and replaced the fairy in her showcase and looked at her palms. "I wish I knew why they did that," she stated, blowing on the palms of her hands in an effort to cool them.

For the past few weeks the palms of Faedra's hands had intermittently seared with a burning sensation, but there was never a rash or any redness, and she couldn't understand what was causing it. She was starting to get concerned about it as the intensity and frequency was increasing. She made a mental note to go and see a doctor; though she wasn't sure what he would say when there was no visible sign that anything was amiss.

"He'd probably just think I was crazy," she thought out loud.

Faen barked, distracting Faedra from her reverie.

"Okay, okay, I'll get ready, just hold your horses." She smiled at him. She knew he loved going to the horse barn with her, and jogging alongside when she took her horse out on a trail ride.

She opened up her clothing closet on the other side of the fireplace, and pulled out her jodhpurs and a t-shirt, then discarded her work clothes to join the disarray already building on her bed. She wiggled into her jodhpurs - it was a good job she was slim, as they didn't leave any room for expansion - pulled on her t-shirt, and wandered over to the dresser. She scooped up the mass of curly red hair that was tumbling down her back and tied it in a ponytail at the nape of her neck then turned and headed for the door.

"Come on, boy. Let's go."

She popped her head in the kitchen doorway on her way out.

"Be back later, Dad. Bye Uncle Leo, bye Nicki, see you soon."

Choruses of have fun and ride carefully resonated from the table, but she had already turned and was heading for the front door.

"Love you guys." she called over her shoulder as she exited into the living room.

Once inside the porch, she pulled on her riding boots and marched out the front door. Wandering round to the right where the climbing rose was blooming in all its glory against the front wall of the cottage. She carefully picked one stem with a bud that was just about to open then strode over to the car, opening the back door for Faen first who jumped in wagging his tail. She got in and laid the rose with care on the passenger seat as if it was the most delicate thing she had ever handled.

Her horse was stabled at a barn just a short drive away on the other side of the village. It only took a few minutes to get there in the car; before she could drive she had ridden her bicycle there come rain or shine. The boarding stables were another of her favorite places, not only because it was home to her horse, but because it, too was an historic building. It used to be an old farm, and the section that housed the stables dated back to when they had to pull the plough by draft horses. The stables lay abandoned for the longest time until the owner decided to retire from the farming business and renovated them to rent them out. The buildings were full of character, and Faedra often found herself imagining what it must have been like to see the heads of all those big draft horses leaning over the stall doors, before the advent of tractors had made them all redundant.

She pulled into the small car park that had been set aside for the boarders, picked up the rose from the passenger seat and hopped out of the car, opening the door for Faen so he could join her. She took a deep breath and looked across the road to where the village church stood proudly in amongst the headstones that were dotted about all over the church grounds. The vicar had once told her that the original part of the church was built in 1160. That was old by anyone's standards, and the two bells that hung in the square bell tower were thought to be the oldest in England. One of them was from 1350 and the other from the fifteenth century. It never ceased to amaze her that something that old could still be standing.

"Come on, let's go say hi to Mum," she said to Faen and looked both ways down the narrow country lane before crossing.

She wandered up the little path that led to the church, and upon reaching the door veered off to the right and followed the path that led behind it. There, spread out before her, was the main part of the graveyard, the section where her mother had been laid to rest nearly twelve years prior.

An odd sensation washed over her and she snapped her head to the left in the direction that it came from. This had been happening more frequently on her recent visits to the churchyard, but yet again there was nothing there except the familiar figure of a black and white border collie, who upon seeing Faedra, came bounding over wagging her tail so vigorously her whole body wiggled in synchronization with it. She assumed the dog belonged to the vicar, but had never seen them together. When the dog reached Faedra she sat down in front of her, looked up and gave her a definitive smile. The first time she had done this Faedra had thought she was baring her teeth in a vicious way, and had been quite unnerved. But it became apparent that the dog was 'smiling', and it was the funniest thing she had ever seen. When the dog 'smiled' she also squinted her eyes in an 'I know something you don't know' fashion.

Faen growled faintly at the other dog as he always did, and in response the collie rubbed her head under Faen's chin just as she always did.

"Be nice, Faen, I think she likes you," Faedra giggled. If a dog could go "urmph" she swore Faen would have. The look of dejection on his face was priceless. It was as if he were an older sibling being forced to play with a younger brother or sister.

She bent down to pat the friendly hound and when she was finished the dog got up and trotted back to where she always sat, in front of the northwest corner of the church. Faedra stepped off the path onto the manicured grass, and meandered her way through the headstones until she reached her mother's.

"Hi, Mum," she said, placing the rose she had picked earlier on top of the stone, replacing the one from a few days before that was now shriveled and dry.

"Just thought I'd pop by and say hello before I take Gypsy out for a ride."

"Good evening, Faedra." A voice called from behind her. She turned.

"Oh hello, Vicar. How are you this evening?"

"Very well thank you, my dear. I see you are off for a ride this fine day," he replied, taking note of Faedra's clothing.

"Sure am, it's a beautiful evening for it."

"Well you have fun, my dear," he said before heading towards the vicarage.

"Excuse me, Vicar," Faedra called out after him.

"Yes, dear?"

"Does that black and white dog belong to you?"

"Which black and white dog, dear?"

"That one…" Faedra's voice trailed off as she noticed the empty space in the direction she was pointing. "The black and white collie that always sits over there."

"Can't say I've ever noticed one, must be a stray, we don't have a dog."

"Oh, never mind then," she said, drawing her eyebrows together as she watched the vicar walk out of sight. She looked over to where she had just pointed, and sure enough the dog was sitting there again like she'd never left.

"Hmm, that's odd," she said, looking down at Faen then shook her head. "Come on let's go get Gypsy tacked up. Bye, Mum, I'll be back soon." She kissed her fingertips and pressed them against the headstone, letting them linger for a moment, before turning toward the path and heading back in the direction of the horse barn.

When she walked back over to the barn, she noticed her friend getting out of a car and wandered over to greet her.

"Hi, Lisa, going out for a ride tonight?" she asked.

"Haven't made my mind up yet, which trail are you thinking of taking?"

"I thought I would go through the woods, it's warm and the shade would keep us cool."

"Nah, then I'll have to say no, Fae. Those woods give me the creeps," Lisa replied with a shudder.

"They do? Why?"

"I can't explain it, I just get a weird feeling in there, freaks me out."

Faedra raised her eyebrows at Lisa's descriptive distaste for the woods, but that wouldn't deter her. She had always loved riding through them and had never felt anything weird, must be Lisa's overactive imagination.

"Okay, no worries, we'll catch up for a ride somewhere else another time then?" Faedra said as she made off in the direction of the paddocks.

"Sure thing, Fae. Catch you later," Lisa was already across the car park and heading toward the stables.

Gypsy was grazing down at the far end of the field when Faedra and Faen reached the gate to her paddock.

"Gypsy!" Faedra called. "Come here girl!"

Gypsy's head popped up and looked in Faedra's direction. It was obvious she recognized her voice. Her horse turned and started to walk toward the gate, then the walk turned to a trot, which turned to a canter until the thunder of her hooves could be heard on the ground. Faedra grinned. She loved that sound. It was a sound she always associated with a feeling of freedom because that's just how she felt when she was on Gypsy's back going that speed. The wind in her face, the thunder of hooves below her, and the countryside zipping past in a blur as they flew like the wind along the trails.

Gypsy was a striking beauty in Faedra's book. Her coloring was classed as blue roan, she had a black coat with white flecks all the way through it that gave her a bluish tinge from a distance. She had a black mane and tail, and a white blaze down the length of her face that had an odd crescent shape to it just below her ears. Three of her legs had white socks that went almost up to her knees, and one back leg had just an 'ankle sock'. Gypsy slowed as she neared the gate, and walked calmly until she was standing just before it. Faedra leaned over the gate and held out a treat for her. Gypsy nuzzled the palm of her hand, gently picking the treat from it.

"Hi, girl," Faedra whispered, rubbing her hand down Gypsy's face. "Ready to go for a ride?"

She climbed up and over the gate, and reached up to put the halter over Gypsy's head. When the halter was fastened, she unbolted the gate and led Gypsy through. Once they reached the stables Faedra tied her to the ring on the wall just next to her stall, and proceeded to groom her. She paid special attention to getting the knots out of her mane and tail. It didn't take long after that before Gypsy was saddled up and ready to go.

Faedra put on her helmet, mounted her horse, and rode out of the yard towards the trailhead, Faen keeping pace behind them. She would have to ride a few yards down the road to reach the entrance to the trail that was on the opposite side of the lane to the barn. The farmer had opened up all of his land to the riders after renovating the stables. He had created several trails that went off in different directions. Faedra's favorite was the one that followed a stream, and then led into and through a thick stand of trees.

The sun was starting to dip in the sultry evening sky, yet another reason she loved the woods. Her ride started out heading towards the sun, and the woods made a handy shade so that she didn't get blinded when the sun dropped to eye level as it was setting. She considered its position in the sky and made a mental note that she had about an hour of riding left before it got too dark. Although Gypsy was very adept at finding her way in the dark, she knew her father would worry and didn't like to give him any reason to.

She always let Gypsy warm up first by walking her for a while, and drifted off into a daydream as she watched the sparkles of light dance in the water of the gently flowing stream to her right. When she was ready Faedra squeezed her calves and made a soft ticking noise with her mouth to ask her horse to move forward into a trot, which Gypsy did quite willingly. The sun was getting brighter by the minute and Faedra was relieved that the opening to the woods was just up ahead.

"Okay, girl, slow it down," she asked, and with a squeeze of her hands on the reins Gypsy responded by coming down into a walk again.

They were at the mouth of the woods and Faedra wanted both of them to adjust their eyes to the decreased light before increasing their speed. She was glad she slowed them down, because as soon as they entered the trees Faedra, at least, was blinded for a moment while her eyes adjusted to the darker surroundings, but she put her trust in her horse to keep on the path until she could see clearly again.

The chinks of light from the sun poked their way through the foliage, creating shards of illuminated, see-through swords, which rained down from high in the branches to the ground below. As they rode through them the shards were distorted, contouring around their bodies. Faedra squeezed Gypsy's sides to push her up into a trot again; she enjoyed picking up the pace in the woods. After a few strides in trot she asked for canter and looked round to check and make sure Faen was keeping up. He was right there on Gypsy's tail, and hardly even panting.

Faedra wondered when Faen was going to start showing his age. He must be nearly thirteen years old by now because he was full-grown when she had found him or rather he had found her, and that was getting old for a dog. Yet he still kept up with Gypsy, and didn't show any signs of slowing down. She looked forward again, not having to worry about guiding her horse through the trail that led through the woods. They had cantered down this path so many times before, but she enjoyed watching the trees fly past, and she thought they must have been half way through by now.

In a split second everything changed. Gypsy came screeching to a halt, throwing Faedra forward and forcing a plume of dust up from the trail. Faedra caught hold of her horse's neck and clung on for dear life until she managed to regain her balance. Adrenaline pumped through her veins as she sat up straight in the saddle and repositioned her feet in the stirrups. She looked all around her in desperation to see if she could spot what had made her horse react so out of character. She could see nothing unusual, but Gypsy continued to be agitated. Her horse started neighing and pawing at the ground, which was creating quite a dust cloud. Faedra became more and more unnerved the more agitated Gypsy became.

"What is it, girl? What's wrong?" she whispered, trying to calm her, but Gypsy just kept getting more and more disturbed.

"Steady, girl. Steady," she took a shorter hold on the reins and attempted to turn her horse around so they could leave. It had become evident that Gypsy was not going to move forward another step.

Just as Faedra thought she was calming Gypsy down, her horse spun and reared all in the same breath. There was nothing Faedra could do. She had lost her footing in the stirrups, and it was such an explosive movement that she was thrown violently from the saddle and hit the ground with so much force it knocked all of the air out of her lungs making a loud 'oomph'.

She could hear the thunder of hooves grow softer and softer as the distance grew between her and Gypsy, but she couldn't move to lift up her head and watch as her horse fled the woods in terror. She couldn't catch her breath either. There was no air getting into to her lungs. She grasped at her chest partly in desperation, partly in fear.

Oh God I can't breathe, what happens if I can't breathe? I'll die. The terrifying thought swam through her head, and she could feel herself starting to panic. Her lips started to tingle, and her fingertips followed suit. She opened her eyes and could make out the shards of light raining down on her, but couldn't focus completely.

"Faen?" she gasped.

A menacing growl resonated from deep within her dog, who she could sense was standing close beside her. She unclasped her arms from her chest and searched with her hands either side of her body for her faithful companion. Relief filled her heart, which was pounding wildly within her ribcage, when she felt his soft fur with her fingertips, and at the same time she was able to catch her first breath.

Her breathing was very shallow at first, but steadily became stronger as the moments passed. When she was able to take a deep breath she did so, and promptly coughed it back up again. She had taken a lung full of the dust that Gypsy had kicked up during her chaotic panic attack and subsequent departure. While lying on the ground she did a mental inventory of bones, moving each limb with caution to see if anything was broken. Nothing seemed to be, so heaving a sigh of relief she pushed herself up into a sitting position.

"Oh good grief, I'm a mess," she groaned, glancing up and down her legs and arms that were now covered in muck and dust. Her clean white t-shirt was more of a khaki color now. There was a tear in her jodhpurs, and her shiny black boots were scuffed and dusty.

She sat still for a moment to check and make sure she did not have any searing pain, she didn't.

"Well I don't think anything's broken, boy," she stated to Faen.

He looked round at her and allowed one wag of his tail in response. Then he turned back to what he was staring at intently in the trees, and continued his ominous growling. Faedra took more notice of it this time because she could see his posture, too, and if he were not her dog she would have been pretty darned frightened of him right at that moment.

Faen stood in a stance that would allow him to pounce at any second. His hackles were standing tall on his back, and his tail was held rigid. He had all his teeth bared. Faedra could hardly recognize this dog as being her Faen. His growl was menacing and it sent chills up her spine.

"What is it, boy?" she whispered, as she looked into the trees where he was staring. Her eyes widened with fear as she caught sight of what Faen would not take his attention from, and gave an involuntary gulp.

"Please tell me those aren't eyes," she stammered. She wasn't sure if she was expecting Faen to reply, but he did with another menacing growl.

There, hiding within the shadows of the trees, were not one, but two sets of what looked like yellow eyes glowing hideously in the darkness.

They could be cats, no they were too tall for cats, and cat's eyes were more rounded. Not dog's eyes either, she pulled in a sharp breath; they looked like smaller versions of human eyes.

"What are they? Who are they?" Faedra asked. Again, Faen growled in response.

The eyes turned to look at each other, and moved up and down as if the owners were nodding to one another in agreement, then they turned back to look in Faedra's direction again.

Faedra felt like a wave of ice cold water had just splashed over her, and she froze where she was, still sitting in the dirt.

Run, Faedra!

A Familiar voice bellowed in her head. Where had she heard that voice before?

Faedra, get up; you have to move, NOW!

She looked all around her, half expecting someone to be hovering above her. Could she get up? She hadn't tried yet. She was feeling very stiff.

FAEDRA RUN!

That did it, pain or no pain she was listening this time, and as if someone had just grabbed her by her shoulders and lifted her off the ground by her bra straps, she suddenly realized she was running as fast as her legs would carry her in the same direction that Gypsy had fled just minutes earlier.

Faen followed closely at her heels. She could hear rustling behind her, and it sounded like it was getting closer. The adrenaline coursing through her veins gave her just enough extra to speed up when she believed she had nothing left, and then they were out of the woods and bathed in the light of the setting sun once again.

Faedra and Faen both ran several yards away from the woods before they looked back. Nothing seemed to be following them now, so they slowed down until they were at a walk. Then it hit her, a stabbing pain in her hip. She stopped and leaned forward, putting her hands on her knees to steady herself while she caught her breath.

"Oh great, I did get hurt," she groaned as her breathing leveled out. She forced herself to stand up and start walking, which quickly turned to a limp.

Up ahead, several people were walking towards them. Faedra recognized one of them as her friend Lisa. As they got closer she could see the worried expressions on their faces, and Lisa broke into a run to get to them sooner.

"Are you okay?" Lisa fussed as she reached Faedra. "Gypsy came charging into the yard like a bat out of hell, sans you, what happened?"

"Something in the woods spooked her. She reared and I just couldn't hang on."

"I told you those woods were creepy," she replied, somewhat too smugly for Faedra's liking.

"Yeah, but we've never had a problem before," Faedra rebutted, "but I dare say I won't be going back through there anytime soon." She looked back towards the woods and shuddered. Just what had she seen in there?

CHAPTER THREE

Gypsy had calmed down by the time Faedra had put her back in the paddock, and she trotted off to join her field buddies seemingly without a care in the world.

"Fickle!" Faedra called out after Gypsy, before limping back to the car and driving home.

She did her best to play down the limp as she walked into the living room upon returning home.

Her dad was relaxing in his chair by the fireplace when she entered, his legs outstretched, his feet resting on a footstool. It was summer so there wasn't a fire burning that night, but it was her father's favorite place to relax. He diverted his eyes from the television to look at her, a smile forming on his lips as it always did until he actually *saw* her. Faedra's face fell as she watched her father's smile vanish, his eyes widen with horror, which then changed to a look of worry.

She could only imagine what she looked like. Covered from head to toe in dirt, clothing torn, and bruises now appearing on her arms. She had a feeling the bruises were going cover her body much more extensively when she got round to peeling her clothes off.

"What on earth happened to you?" he cried.

"I'm okay, Dad," she lied. In reality she felt like she'd just gone ten rounds with a heavyweight boxer. Her body ached all over.

"Well you don't look okay. Are you going to tell me what happened?"

Faedra shuffled over to the sofa, plunked herself down rather unceremoniously, and winced as she made contact with the cushions.

"Something spooked Gypsy in the woods. She reared and threw me," Faedra explained with indifference. She thought it best to leave out the bit about the glowing yellow eyes and Faen's distinct aversion to them at this juncture.

"Well that's not like her, she's never thrown you before and you've been through those woods hundreds of times."

"I know, Dad, but I have myself to blame for becoming complacent with her. She's always so sensible, I forget that she is still an animal and therefore unpredictable."

Faen barked.

"Okay, boy, apart from you. You are definitely the least unpredictable animal I have ever met in my life."

She sensed that he seemed satisfied by that remark as he sat down beside her.

"You know, Fae, I could swear sometimes that dog understands every word you say."

"You've noticed too? I thought I was just imagining it. Anyway, I'm going to take a bath," she eased herself up off the sofa with yet another grimace.

"There's some Epsom salts in the cabinet, should help ease some of the soreness, but I think you're probably going to be a bit stiff for a few days."

"Thanks, Dad."

"Fae?"

"Yes, Dad."

"Take it easy, darling, I don't want to lose you too." His poignant statement was not lost on her; she had always been very conscious to avoid doing anything that would make her dad worry.

"You won't, Dad, I promise," she said with a reassuring smile.

Faedra made it to the bathroom rather more slowly than usual, reached over to turn on the taps, and sprinkled the Epsom salts under the steaming flow of hot water. She lifted her t-shirt over her head with care and peeled off the jodhpurs, discarding them in the laundry basket. She wasn't sure if they were salvageable, but it was worth a try. She turned her attention to the mirror.

"Oh my goodness," she gasped as her battered reflection stared back at her. Nearly her entire body was covered in patches of red, the first stage of a bruise, and she thanked her lucky stars that she was sensible enough to wear a helmet, it could have been a lot worse. "Those bruises are going to be sore," she groaned.

After a few more minutes of closer examination her bath was ready. She slipped out of her underwear and dipped her toes in the water to make sure it was not too hot. It wasn't, so she eased herself down, letting out a sigh of comfort as she sank up to her neck in the warm steamy water. She could feel the healing warmth envelope her body, seeping into her muscles, and after several minutes the soreness ebbed away.

The candle she had lit when she started the bath was flickering in front of the mirror giving the appearance of there being two of them. She watched the glowing flame send a soothing warm light throughout the bathroom. A few more minutes passed, her mind drifted, and her eyelids grew heavy.

In an instant she was back in the woods again, fear coursing through her veins. Her eyes under their lids darted about erratically, and her breathing quickened. Faen, who was laying the other side of the bathroom door, could sense something was wrong. He sat up with an urgency and scratched at the door.

She was once again staring at the frightful yellow eyes, glowing with ominous intent, hiding in the shadows of the trees. Her body turned ice cold with trepidation once more.

Faedra, Run!

Her eyes flew open and she pushed herself up in the bath sending water splashing over the sides. Disoriented she looked around with trepidation then sighed with relief when she realized she was still in the security of her bathroom.

"Mum," she whispered to herself. "It was Mum's voice in the woods."

Faen scratched on the door again.

"It's okay, boy. It was just a dream."

She hefted herself out of the bath, and after drying and dressing into her pajamas, trudged down the hall. It was odd how her bedroom was located within the cottage. After the renovations there was no entrance to her room from the new part of the house. To access it, one had to walk down the back stairs, come through the kitchen and dining room, and walk up another set of stairs that led only to her bedroom. The other original bedroom, next to hers, would have been accessed through her room when the cottage was built, but that door had been sealed off long ago, and had its own access from the new side of the house. Usually this would not have been an issue, but tonight as stiff and sore as she felt, it was.

It took Faedra ages to hobble down one set of stairs and then up another, and when she opened her door she let out a loud groan. She had completely forgotten about the mess on her bed that had been dumped there earlier. Scuttling over to her bed she pushed it all onto the floor, she'd deal with it tomorrow. She flopped on the bed, sore and exhausted.

"Night, Faen," she whispered, and was asleep almost before her head hit the pillow.

***

The sun shining in through the window woke Faedra the following morning. Her curtains, although pretty, didn't do anything helpful to keep the room dark once the sun had decided to peek over the horizon. She opened her eyes and stretched, a smile crept across her lips when she realized what day it was. It was Saturday, and she was taking her two best friends, make that three best friends if you included Faen, to Strawberry Fair.

As soon as Faedra had passed her driving test she had bought a car, albeit a bit of an old banger. She was so excited at the prospect of being able to drive herself to Strawberry Fair that she had been marking the days off on her calendar. When she'd mentioned it to her friends, they had wanted to go with her, so she had been looking forward to this day for months.

Strawberry Fair was held in Cambridge, about an hour and a half drive from her home. It was the largest one-day festival held in Cambridge, and had been held annually for over thirty years now. It was first started as an 'alternative' festival, a bit like a renaissance fair she imagined, but now it was very much like most other festivals held around the country, although she was secretly hoping there were still some vendors of the more 'mystical' variety, something that has always interested her. Maybe she could get her palms read.

There would be all kinds of arts and crafts, music, food, and shows. Thousands of people from all over the country converged on Cambridge for that single day a year, and this year she was going to be one of them. Eager to get going, she threw back the covers and jumped out of bed. Then something struck her as odd. She didn't hurt.

She scanned both of her arms, no big ugly black and blue bruises, just a little redness in some areas. She walked around for a few steps. There was a very faint aching in her hip, but nothing like the throbbing pain of last night. Confused, she walked to the mirror and pulled her top up to reveal the skin beneath, nothing but patches of a reddish tinge reflected back at her. Could Epsom salts do that? She wondered as she kept checking for bruising and finding nothing. Coming to the conclusion that she can't have been as badly bruised as she had first thought. She put it to the back of her mind and wandered over to her closet, rummaged around for a moment and grabbed a pair of shorts, and a sleeveless top with thin straps. It was going to be a warm day, and now that there were no hideous bruises to hide, she could dress accordingly.

Once dressed, Faedra skipped down the stairs and into the kitchen. Her father was leaning against the counter waiting for his toast to pop out of the toaster. He looked at her in astonishment.

"Must have been the Epsom salts," she gave as explanation to answer the obvious confusion in his expression.

He raised his eyebrows. "I guess so."

She grabbed a slice of toast that had just popped up out of the toaster.

"Hey that's mine, young lady," Henry exclaimed.

"We're off, I'll see you later tonight. Enjoy yourself on the boat and give my love to Uncle Leo and Nicki." She grinned her cheeky grin and planted a kiss on his cheek. "Love you."

"Have fun, and drive carefully," he called after her, but she was already halfway to the living room. Henry shook his head with a big smile on his face. His daughter was growing up fast, and turning into a fine young lady.

***

Faedra pulled up outside her friend, Amy's house. She had arranged to pick Zoë up from there too. Zoë lived close to Amy, so it was on the way. She honked the horn to let them know she was there. A couple of minutes passed, and just as she was about to honk again the front door opened and her two friends appeared. Amy was a little shorter than Zoë who was about the same height as Faedra. They were all roughly the same build, but had very different features. Amy had white blonde hair, cropped into a short spiky style. She had blue eyes and pale skin, but unlike Faedra, not a freckle to be seen. Something that Faedra couldn't help but be envious of. Amy was a party waiting to happen, there was never a dull moment when she was around.

Zoë on the other hand, had long sleek dark brown hair that flowed down her back and shone in the sunlight. Her olive toned skin complimented her warm green/brown eyes and she always looked great in anything she wore. Between the three of them they had all the hair colors covered: blonde, brunette, and redhead.

Faedra could see the excitement in their smiles as they made their way down the garden path to the car.

"Hi, Fae," Amy chirped as she took her assumed position in the front passenger seat.

Zoë didn't hesitate jumping in the back seat beside Faen. She loved Faen almost as much as Faedra. It seemed to Faedra the feeling was mutual.

"How's my boy today?" Zoë said as she mussed Faen's ears, and planted a big kiss on his nose. Faedra was watching her in the rearview mirror and a big grin spread across her lips.

"Hi guys," Faedra said. "Well we've got a great day for it."

The journey to Cambridge flew by. They fell into the usual girlie chatter and didn't stop talking for the entire drive there. Amy told them in great detail about her latest conquest, and Faedra had to admit he did sound rather nice and was looking forward to meeting him. Zoë was already in a relationship and she was perfectly happy. They had been together since the beginning of high school, and at this point it didn't look like that was going to change any time soon.

Faedra hadn't yet met anyone she felt any connection to. Although she had been asked out on numerous dates, she had always politely declined. She had a feeling that when the right person came along she would know in an instant, and just didn't want to waste her time, or his, when she knew it wouldn't go any further than the first date.

Cars started to slow several miles out from Cambridge with all the festival traffic trying to make its way into the city.

They sat in traffic for what seemed like half the day, but was, in fact, only about half an hour until they were eventually ushered into a huge field. They followed the line of cars in front of them until they found a parking space.

They got out of the car and mingled in with the crowd of people heading towards the entrance to the festival. The deep bass of music off in the distance resounded all around them. As they got closer to the festival the music became more distinctive, and the crowd got larger. Faedra couldn't help but get completely caught up in the atmosphere. She soaked it all in, observing with interest the people in the crowd surrounding her. Every age range, from babies in pushchairs to older retirees, were present.

It seemed to her that there were three categories of people attending the festival. Those who dressed in ordinary clothing like her and her friends. Those that were dressed somewhat hippie-ish, with long hair, beards, and psychedelic t-shirts emblazoned with the 'peace' sign. And those who were just all out eccentric, wearing anything from renaissance clothing to cross-dressing. One couple that walked past her were dressed in silver clothing, wearing pink wigs, with one sporting devil horns and the other a tiara. Faedra guessed they were using the 'good versus evil' take on their costumes.

Finally, they were through the gates, and the festival spread out in all its enticing glory before them. There were hundreds of tents, housing vendors of all descriptions, and from this angle they could see at least two stages where bands were playing live music.

"Where do we go first?" Amy asked, looking in all directions.

"Well, we could start off in that direction and make our way round. We've got all day," Zoë responded.

"That sounds like a plan," Faedra agreed.

They headed off toward a stage where a band was playing some type of folk music. The band called 'Hogwash' had attracted quite a crowd. People were standing around watching as well as sitting down in the grass. Most were drinking beer. After watching them for a while, Faedra grinned at her friend Amy who was wiggling her hips in time with the movement. It had always been virtually impossible for Amy to keep still if music was playing. Even in the car she jiggled about in her seat to whatever song was blasting from the radio.

A few songs later they decided to move on, and spent some time glancing at the vendors as they walked past. There were arts and crafts of all types. Faedra was interested in the hand made jewelry. Zoë was more into the candles and incense vendors while Amy was attracted by anything pink.

"I'm hungry," Zoë mentioned after they had been window-shopping for an hour. "Can we find a food tent?"

"That one over there looks fairly innocuous," Faedra said, pointing in the direction of a hotdog and hamburger stall. She was starting to get a little disappointed, she had been hoping to see lots of 'mystical' stalls, but not a *Gypsy Rose Lee* was to be seen so far.

They wandered over to the food stall and tucked into some not too awful hamburgers. Faedra always thought it was a bit of potluck, putting your digestive health in the hands of a food vendor at an outdoor event. After they had finished eating, Amy wanted to find another stage and listen to some more music. They all headed off toward the sound of music blaring behind a few more of the vendor's tents. Then it caught Faedra's eye; a sign that read *Runes read by Rose, Let the stones guide you.*

"Hey, guys, I'm just going to go over there," she pointed towards the tent she had just spotted.

"Oh, Fae, don't waste your money, everyone knows they are all frauds," Zoë cautioned.

"It's just a bit of fun, I'll catch up with you, I've got my cell phone with me if I can't find you."

"Okay, we'll see you in a bit, but your wasting your money," Zoë said, as she and Amy started off in the direction of the music.

Faedra wandered over to the tent. Most of the vendor's tents were only enclosed on three sides, but this one was enclosed on all sides, allowing privacy to the person getting a reading she assumed. She wasn't quite sure what to do when she arrived at the tent. It wasn't as if there was a door to knock on before she entered. She didn't want to be rude and burst in on someone if they were having their runes read. She stood outside the tent for a moment contemplating the situation, and then decided she would just call out. If anyone was in there, they would hear her and let her know if they were busy or not.

"Hello?" Faedra called next to the material that made up one of the tent walls. "Is anyone in there?"

"Hello," came the voice from inside, "please, come in."

Faen whined. "It's okay, boy. You stay out here. I won't be long."

Faedra did as the voice said and pulled the material aside to enter. The inside of the tent was exactly as she would have imagined a *Gypsy Rose Lee* tent to look like. There was the strong smell of incense burning, which she saw was coming from a little table in the corner that also housed the obligatory crystal ball. Rose was seated at a small card table in the center of the tent that had a purple, crushed velvet cloth edged with a fringe draped over it. The chairs were just ordinary plastic folding ones that probably came in a set with the table. Faedra smiled, Zoë was more than likely right, but she thought it would be good for a giggle, so she decided to stay.

Rose got up from the table and held her hand out for Faedra. Faedra had to admit she was slightly surprised because Rose did not fit the *Gypsy Rose Lee* stereotype she had created in her mind. Yes, she was dressed in a gypsy-ish way with a long floating skirt and billowy white blouse, but she was younger than Faedra had imagined. She had expected a much older woman, possibly with her fair share of wrinkles, but the lady facing her right now didn't look much older than thirty. She had a fresh rosy complexion with beautiful green eyes, and long wavy dark hair hidden partially by a deep red headscarf.

"Hello, I'm Rose," she said brightly as they shook hands. "Please don't tell me yours," she continued as Faedra opened her mouth to return the greeting.

"Err, hello," Faedra responded.

Rose gestured for Faedra to take a seat, and then picked a small sign off the table that read *Reading in session* and hung it on a hook that was on one of the tent posts. Once she returned to the table she made herself comfortable and picked up a small black velvet pouch that was lying in the center.

"Now, I want you to think of a question or a situation you would like guidance on, you must not tell me what it is, then pick out six Rune stones and hand them to me," Rose explained as she opened the pouch and held the open end to Faedra.

Faedra thought carefully for a moment before dipping her fingers into the pouch and pulled out the first stone, handing it to Rose who placed it onto the crushed velvet tablecloth. She did this five more times until all six stones had been extracted from their pouch. Faedra watched as Rose carefully arranged them in the shape of a cross. Rose then pulled the strings on the pouch to close it, and placed it to one side.

Faedra watched as Rose examined the Runes intently, and stifled a giggle when she thought back to Zoë's remark. Rose was certainly putting on a good show, umming and ahhing for several minutes, but Faedra could start to feel a distinct shift in the once pleasant, if not slightly kooky atmosphere in the tent. Suddenly there was a very tense sensation surrounding her, and she drew her eyebrows together in a frown.

Rose's eyes widened. "No, this can't be," she mumbled to herself, "it's just a legend." Then she drew her burning gaze from the Rune stones to Faedra.

Faedra shifted uncomfortably in her seat.

"What do you see? What's just a legend?" she asked.

Rose didn't speak for a moment.

She was contemplating something important. "You," she stated bluntly.

Faedra laughed, it escaped before she had chance to stifle it. "I'm sorry but I think my friend was right, I'll not waste any more of your time."

She started to get up to leave but Rose beat her to it. Before Faedra even got her butt off the seat Rose stood up, rounded the table, and was standing behind her. She let out a gasp.

"What?" Faedra demanded, turning in her seat to see Rose eyeing the back of her neck. "It's a birthmark, what of it? Look this is ridiculous, I'll give you ten out of ten for the dramatics, but I was hoping for a serious reading," she stood up and spun round so that she was now facing Rose.

"You have no idea who you are, do you Faedra?" Rose whispered.

"I know exactly who I am, thank you very much," she stated obstinately, "and I know who you are, you are a fraud… Hey, how did you know my name? I never told you my name." An uneasy feeling started to well up in the pit of her stomach.

"How old are you?" Rose asked.

"Seventeen," Faedra snapped.

Rose closed her eyes, dropped her head, and let out a heavy sigh. She had already said too much.

"Tell me how you know my name," Faedra demanded, "and why you're so interested in my birthmark!"

"I can't, you are not of age yet. I've already said too much."

"Not of age yet? What does that mean?" Faedra demanded again, she was starting to get annoyed.

"I never imagined I would be in this position. I thought it was all just a myth, but our people have a pact with yours. You will find out soon enough. Sorry, Faedra, I can say no more, you must go." She moved over to the entrance and held it open.

Faedra glared at Rose as she brushed past her.

"Faedra?"

"What?" Faedra snapped.

"Good luck."

Faedra looked at her and shook her head. "Come on, Faen, let's get out of here."

She stomped off in the direction of the music to find her friends. She was almost too angry to notice the burning in the palms of her hands until it got too unbearable, so she stopped at a drinks stall to ask for some ice.

"I don't know who I am indeed," she muttered as she held a couple of ice cubes that melted instantaneously.

"Who did she think she was anyway?" she grumbled to Faen who was keeping very close to her side, much closer than usual. He was always with her, but most of the time kept several feet away, at the moment he was glued to her leg.

Faedra continued her mutterings until she found her friends dancing in a crowd that had gathered in front of a stage playing more modern music this time.

"How'd it go?" Amy shouted above the music when Faedra reached them.

"Zoë was right, she was a fraud."

"Well I hope you didn't give her any money," Zoë shouted.

"Didn't get a chance to, she kicked me out before I even got a reading," Faedra complained.

"What?" Amy and Zoë shouted in unison. "Why did she do that?"

"She said something about me not being of age and not knowing who I was." It sounded ridiculous to Faedra even as she said the words.

"See told you," Zoë chimed in, "frauds, the lot of them. Well don't let it spoil your day, Fae."

Faedra decided she wouldn't, and joined her friends in a dance. The rest of the day passed without incident and they arrived home safe, but exhausted. After dropping her friends off, she pulled in her driveway. Her Dad was still out and she hoped he was enjoying himself with Uncle Leo and Nicki after a day on the boat.

She darted up to her room, ran around the bed to her dresser, and grabbed her small hand held mirror. Holding it up in front of her, she turned her back to the vanity mirror on her dresser and examined her birthmark. She'd never paid it much attention before because it was at the nape of her neck between her shoulders. It wasn't easy for her to see, and as her hair usually covered it she forgot it was there most of the time. Today she had put her hair up because it was so thick; it was like wearing a scarf on a sunny day. Now she could see it clearly in the reflection in the mirror.

She leaned closer to get a better look and her eyes widened with surprise.

"Wow it must have grown, I can't remember it looking that big before, what does it remind me of?" She drew her eyes away from the mirror to look straight ahead at her collection, and then reverted them back to her reflection again, narrowing them as she did.

"It's a fairy."

CHAPTER FOUR

The next couple of nights Faedra did not get much sleep, it was fitful at best. The events of the past few weeks, and more recently the past couple of days, kept repeating in her dreams and she would wake often, usually in a cold sweat.

She dragged herself out of bed as she had done the previous morning, and all but crawled over to the dresser. She thought about calling in sick, but integrity fought against her and won.

"Urgh," she groaned when greeted by her reflection in the mirror. Dark circles framed her once sparkling eyes that were now dull and lackluster.

"If this carries on too much longer, I'm going to have to steal some sleeping pills from somewhere," she croaked to Faen.

She fiddled with her makeup and after applying a healthy dose of concealer and foundation, started to look a little less like the monster from the deep. Faen, who was sitting beside her, looked up at her with what she considered was a look of concern.

"It's okay, boy, I'll be fine. Not sure what's going on, but I'm sure it will pass." She said it more as reassurance for herself than anything else. After she was done putting on the finishing touches of her 'disguise' she wandered over to the closet and picked out something smart but casual for work.

She had a job at a company that shipped freight all over the world. It was located at the local airport. It wasn't a large airport but did have flights to Scotland, Ireland and various European countries. She had flown out of there herself in the past, on holiday to Spain. The view from her office almost made the abuse she was dealt worth it. It looked over the entire airfield, and she could see the planes take off and land all throughout the day, but she hated her boss.

Jerry Thompson was the most unpleasant person she had ever met. It wasn't just his very poor attention to personal hygiene, but he also seemed to go out of his way to make her life a misery, and quite obviously enjoyed doing so. She often wondered why she put up with it and didn't just leave. She wasn't a quitter that was why.

Dressed and caked in make up she almost stumbled down the stairs to the dining room. Her Dad was already sitting at the table in the kitchen having his breakfast when she walked in.

"Cup of tea, Fae?" he asked. "God you look awful," he continued when he looked up to see his daughter.

Faedra groaned inwardly, her attempts at applying make up hadn't had the desired effect.

"Yes please, and thanks I love you too," she replied testily to his question and subsequent observation. She was never her best when tired. A bear with a sore head was an apt comparison.

Henry poured her a cup of tea as she joined him at the table.

"Are you okay, darling? Maybe you should call in sick today," he suggested.

"I haven't slept very well the past couple of days. I'll be fine though, I'm not about to give Mr. Thompson any more reasons to pick on me than he already feels he has."

She ate her breakfast in silence. Today was not going to be a good day and she could already feel herself wishing it were over. Apart from the fact that she felt like a zombie and probably looked like an extra from the *Thriller* video, it was also the anniversary of her mother's death. She closed her eyes for a moment and gave herself an inward pep talk.

Come on Fae pull yourself together, it's only twenty-four hours and then it will be over for another year.

She always spent some time at her mother's grave on the anniversary of her death. It was a tradition of hers that she had started some years ago now. She would take a blanket, a small picnic, sit down next to the headstone, and talk to her mum about anything and everything. Somewhere deep inside she knew her mum was listening. She had to believe it, it was one of the things that kept her sane.

***

"Morning, Faedra, you look like crap," Mr. Thompson greeted her as she walked in the office dead on nine o'clock, "another minute and you'd have been late," he continued in his smarmy voice as he looked down at his wrist and tapped his watch.

She took a deep breath and bit her lip. "Morning, Mr. Thompson," she sighed as she took her seat behind her desk.

Mr. Thompson was a greasy looking middle-aged man. He was fat and balding with a shiny head usually covered in beads of sweat. He had beady little eyes that were positioned far too close together on his face to be natural, and for some unknown reason he decided it looked good to have a beard. Faedra had felt her stomach lurch on several occasions when he had come back from lunch with bits of greasy food stuck in it, and imagined him in his office picking bits off for an afternoon snack. She stifled a shudder. His clothing was always dirty, especially his shirts that, more often than not, had splotches of spilled food on them. It was as if he didn't know what a washing machine was, or cared.

Everyone in the company hated him, but they were relieved when she started working there because his attention was now directed completely on her, as it was on all the new employees before her, and would be until some poor soul was hired in below her. Something that wasn't likely to happen, as her position was the lowest on the totem pole.

Faedra was the receptionist for the freight company, so her main job focus was to answer the phones, direct people to various departments, and greet people who walked through the door. She was the first person you saw when you walked in, and the last when you walked out. Mr. Thompson did throw in some filing for her to do for good measure. Just such a task would set the wheels in motion for Faedra to become very aware that something was seriously amiss.

"Faedra Bennett," Mr. Thompson snapped, making her jump. She had her back to him with her hands in the filing cabinet; putting away the load of files he had given her just a few minutes ago. "How many times do I have to tell you? ANSWER THE PHONE IN ONE RING!" he shouted, making her jump once more.

The whole office fell silent, and all heads turned in her direction.

"But, Mr. Thompson, I have my hands in the filing cabinet filing the records you just gave me and the nearest phone is all the way over there," she pointed to a desk a good twenty feet away.

"I don't care about your petty excuses, girl, do what I ask you to or I'll write you up. DO I MAKE MYSELF UNDERSTOOD?"

Faedra could feel herself get hot, and her cheeks redden. She was not used to getting shouted at, and tears pricked behind her eyes, but she'd be darned if she was going to show this bully that he'd upset her. She certainly was not about to cry in front of the whole office, so she managed to blink them back.

"Sorry, Mr. Thompson, it won't happen again," she said softly.

"Just make sure it doesn't girl," he gloated and turned to leave. "Oh, and I need the Hodgkin's report too."

"Yes, Mr. Thompson."

She heard him mutter *stupid girl* as he stormed off in the direction of his office. Heaving a heavy hearted sigh, she finished the filing and wandered past all of her co-workers - who were looking at her with sympathy - to her desk at the end of the room. She smiled sheepishly at the ones who made eye contact with her, but most just averted their gazes as she passed.

She had only been in front of her computer for a few minutes, not time enough to calm herself down yet, before she heard the familiar weighty footsteps stomping down the office towards her. Within seconds his hefty form was taking up the space in front of her desk. Looking up warily, she grimaced at his demeanor. His face was almost puce; she thought he was going to have a heart attack right there and then. He better not because there was no way she was giving *that* mouth-to-mouth. The thought made her incredibly nauseous.

"Did I not make myself clear, Girl?" he shouted.

"I'm sorry, Mr. Thompson, I don't understand what you mean."

"When I tell you I need a report, I need it NOW. I do not expect to have to wait until Christmas! Trust me to hire another imbecile!" he bellowed, before snatching the report that Faedra had already printed - just not gotten it to him yet - off the printer and stormed off back down the office again.

Faedra was shaken; she struggled to force back more tears, but this time they were tears of anger. Had she ever been this angry before? She couldn't remember. Her whole body was trembling and her palms that were resting face down on some paperwork were burning worse than they ever had before. This time it was not just a sensation, it was downright painful. She lifted her hands to blow on them, and as she did her eyes widened in horror and confusion. There on the paper were two scorch marks right where her hands had been.

She scanned the office to see if anyone had noticed, but everyone had their heads down attempting to look like they were working industriously. Balling up the paper, she threw it in the bin and went to the rest room to run her hands under some cold water. She was getting very concerned about her hands now. What had just happened was definitely not normal; she also knew that she couldn't tell anyone, they would think her crazy for sure.

For the rest of the day Faedra managed to keep herself under the radar until it was time to go home. An enormous weight lifted from her shoulders the minute she walked out the door. She felt as light as a feather as if she would float away on even the most delicate of breezes.

***

After going home to change and pick up Faen, and her picnic basket, Faedra pulled into the church car park. There were no other cars there, which suited her. People often gave her funny looks as they walked by when she was nattering away to no one visible. She pulled her blanket and picnic basket from the trunk, and strolled towards the graveyard.

It was a beautiful, warm evening with not a cloud in the sky. There was a slight breeze that ruffled the leaves on the trees. The graveyard was about an acre or two in size and framed on three sides by ancient oak trees, with the church standing proudly on the remaining side. She knew that the vicarage was behind the trees to her right and believed that there were fields behind the other trees. It was hard to see through them, not because they were a thick stand of trees, but because they were covered with their summer foliage.

Faedra was in a daze as she meandered her way through the headstones. She had been here to visit her mum so many times that she thought she could probably find her headstone blind folded by now. It was just as well, she was so tired this evening she didn't have her wits about her, and felt like she was on autopilot navigating her way through them.

The friendly black and white collie had spotted them as they came through the gate from the car park and bounded up to greet her and Faen, giving Faedra her usual toothy grin. The collie and Faen went through their established routine of him growling softly at her, while she rubbed her head against his chin in response. This time though, instead of her running off to sit in her usual spot after Faedra had petted her, she stayed with them and followed behind until they made it to Lillith's grave.

"Here we are again, boy," she sighed, her voice weighted down with sadness.

She set down the picnic basket, threw out the blanket on the ground and sat down on it, leaning up against her mother's headstone, legs outstretched in front of her. She patted her hands on the blanket either side of her legs.

"Come on you two, you can join me you know," she said to the two dogs that were standing either side of the blanket and looking at her with an understanding she couldn't quite figure out. They did as she asked and lay down next to her, putting a head on each of Faedra's thighs so that they were nose-to-nose. The 'sibling rivalry' was completely gone, and they both let out a sad sounding whine in unison.

"Hey, you two, I'm okay," Faedra ran her hands over both of their soft silky heads and they didn't take their eyes off her.

Faedra let out a heavy sigh and leaned her head back to rest it against the cold hard granite of the headstone and closed her eyes. It felt nice and cool against the balmy warm of the evening air. A few minutes passed and she said nothing, but listened to the sounds of nature surrounding her. She could hear the dogs breathing, and felt their hot breath on her hands that were now resting on her thighs. The birds chirped in the trees behind her, and in the distance she could hear a horse whinny from the stables across the road.

A crunching on the gravel path prompted her to open her eyes. It was the vicar and he was heading in her direction.

"Good evening, Faedra, I thought I might find you here this evening," he said with a knowing smile.

"Hello, Vicar," she replied.

"Are you feeling alright, my dear?" he asked, his eyebrows pulled together to form a frown.

"I'm fine," she lied, "haven't been sleeping very well the past couple of nights and right now I feel a little sad, but I'll be fine."

He seemed satisfied with her answer and smiled again. "Well, if you need me dear, you know where to find me. Say hello to your mother for me won't you."

"I will, Vicar, thank you."

He turned and headed towards the church, and she watched as he disappeared behind it, closed her eyes again and sat in silence for a few more minutes. She was trying to clear her head before she spoke to her mum, but the more she tried the more out of focus she became until she could hold it in no longer. A wave of emotion swept over her and she burst into tears. She was tired and had had an awful day.

"Mum, I miss you so much," she sobbed. "All this strange stuff is happening to me, I don't know why and I don't know what to do about it. I don't feel like I can tell anyone. I mean, I think I'm going crazy, so I can't imagine what other people would think. They'd probably lock me up and throw away the key."

Tears tumbled down Faedra's face. The eyes in the woods, the fortune-teller at the fair, the abuse by Mr. Thompson, her hands, and the fact she missed her mother desperately, all came flooding out. She buried her face in her hands; her body was wracked with emotions that were out of her control for the moment. The tears were relentless, and she felt powerless to stop them. She was hoping a good cry would make her feel better.

A cold wet nose nudged her elbow. She ignored it. Faen nudged her again; this time she took her hands away from her face, which was now red and blotchy. She could see the blurry outline of her dog looking at her with sadness in his eyes too.

She wrapped her arms around his neck, just like the first time she had met him. Buried her face in his soft fur and accepted the comfort she felt when she did so.

"I wish she could give me some kind of sign that she was still with me," Faedra said into his neck. "Faen, sometimes I feel so alone."

He whimpered in response, she still had her head buried in his fur. She didn't have the strength, just yet, to leave the security and comfort she felt when he was close to her, and he was not about to move a muscle until Faedra had calmed down.

A few more moments of sobbing passed, and the shudders rippling through her body started to ebb. Her breathing became less ragged, and she pulled herself from Faen to wipe the tears from her eyes with a tissue she had grabbed from the picnic basket. When her eyes began to focus, and the drumming in her ears from the pulse of her heartbeat calmed, she heard a familiar sound that she hadn't heard for a very long time.

She looked up and gasped. Sitting on the headstone directly in front of her was a bird, not just any old bird, her mum's favorite bird. Its name escaped her at that moment, but she knew it was fairly rare and not seen in this area very often. It looked directly at her and sang its beautiful lilting song.

A surge of comfort swept through Faedra at the sight. It was the sign she had asked for.

"I knew it, look, Faen," she said, pointing at the bird. "It's Mum's favorite bird, she sent me a sign, she is with me," she looked up heavenward. "Thanks, Mum, that's just what I needed."

Faedra felt her spirits lift exponentially in comparison to how she felt when she first entered the graveyard a little while before. She regained her appetite, and decided it was time to eat the sandwiches she had packed into her picnic basket. Straightening herself up she sat cross-legged on the blanket and placed the basket in front of her.

The dogs both sat up and looked expectantly at the picnic basket that was now positioned between them.

"Don't worry you two, there's something in here for you as well," she said with a smile, the first one she had managed all day.

She pulled out a couple of ham sandwiches and passed one each to Faen, and the collie. They wolfed theirs down in seconds and looked again at Faedra, and then at the basket.

"That's your lot, you greedy buggars," she laughed and pulled out an egg sandwich for herself. She loved egg sandwiches they were her favorites. Her mum used to make them for her when she was a child, so it was only fitting that she would bring one to eat when she visited her.

The little bird sat perched on the headstone the entire time, and Faedra threw it a few crumbs. It hopped down onto the ground and finished up the crumbs that had been offered it.

A few moments passed, and their picnic was finished. Faedra felt like a huge weight had lifted off her shoulders. She leaned back up against the cool granite of her mother's headstone and closed her eyes again. She didn't want to leave just yet, although she was incredibly tired.

She wasn't sure how long she'd been asleep when she was woken suddenly by a low carnal growl that she recognized instantly as being the same as that time in the woods a few days ago. Her eyes snapped open and fear whipped through her. She felt disoriented for a second because it was almost dark. That odd light just after the sun goes down and the night sets in.

Faen and the collie were both standing to her left; their hackles were raised, and they were postured ready to fight. Faedra noticed the oddest thing at that moment. The collie was looking at Faen, and growling in different tones. Faen returned the collie's gaze, and growled back in different tones, also. Were they talking to each other? It certainly looked like it. Faedra watched in amazement as the two dogs seemingly had a conversation right before her eyes, then they turned their attention on her and she almost jumped.

The collie barked at her, it was an insistent bark, like she was instructing her to do something, but what? Faedra didn't talk dog. The unusual scene unfolding before her almost made her forget what was causing it in the first place, until the collie looked back in the same direction as Faen and continued her deep menacing growl. The two of them looked ferocious, sending shivers down Faedra's back. Although Faedra was loathed to, she couldn't stop herself looking into the trees, and the familiar icy cold feeling washed over her again.

"Oh no, not again," she whispered to herself as she bent down and scooped up her blanket and picnic basket, ready to make a quick exit. "What *are* those things?"

She was watching trance-like at what looked like the same pairs of eyes she had seen in the woods the other day. Only this time there were three pairs of them. The collie barked a response then looked at Faen and snapped a bark at him, too. He turned and all but pushed Faedra in the direction of the car park. She snapped out of her trance and picked up the pace, running as fast as she could while dodging between the headstones. The older ones were dotted randomly all over their exit path. Symmetry was not something that had been adopted in the olden days, but she wished for it now. She bashed her hip into the corner of one as she miscalculated its position when running past it.

"Ouch. This is getting beyond a joke," she cursed to herself, not daring to look back incase those things were chasing her. She could hear the collie's growl getting fainter as they drew closer and closer to her car. They reached it, but Faedra couldn't find her keys. She had tossed them in the picnic basket when they'd arrived, and now was frantically feeling around in it, trying to grab them.

Faen barked several times in quick succession.

"I'm trying, Faen, I know they're in here somewhere." Her heart was racing, she didn't know if those things were close or not. Her fingertips brushed over the cold metal of her keys. "Got them," she exclaimed as she pulled her hand out of the basket clutching onto her car keys. She opened the door and let Faen in the back, threw the basket and blanket on the passenger seat, then jumped in herself and put the keys in the ignition.

"No no no, don't do this to me now," she cried as she turned the keys, and the car responded with a splutter. "Come on, Sally, you can do it. You have to get us out of here," she coaxed her car as she turned the key again. Still there was nothing but a splutter. "I promise I'll never call you an old banger ever again if you start for me now," she pleaded and turned the keys once more. The engine spluttered to life.

"Yes! Thank you," she patted the steering wheel.

Faedra revved the engine a couple of times and then put it into gear and drove out of the car park, spraying gravel out behind her as she did.

"Sorry, Vicar," she cried, as if he were standing right there and had witnessed her speedy exit. "Thanks, Sally, you have my word, I'll never call you an old banger again."

Faedra had named her car when she first bought it. Her dad had thought it cute and her uncle had made fun of her, but she didn't care. She heaved a sigh of relief as she put more and more distance between her and the church.

"I hope I'm going to get some answers soon, my life is getting just a little too weird of late," she thought out loud.

***

The next morning she wasn't surprised to see that the bruise that had been forming on her hip, where she had bashed it against a headstone during last night's getaway, had all but vanished. A slight reddening of the area was all that remained.

She got ready for work. Only another couple of days and it would be her birthday. She was so pleased that it fell on a Saturday this year. She was planning an evening out with Zoë and Amy, and was looking forward to going out and having some fun with her friends.

CHAPTER FIVE

The sun peeking through the curtains awoke Faedra on the morning of her eighteenth birthday. She stretched, and rubbed the sleep from her eyes as she turned over to look at the time on the clock that was sitting on her nightstand. It told her that it was six thirty in the morning.

"Urgh it's still early," she moaned.

Faen was lying on the rug next to her bed and stirred when he heard her move. He sat up and looked at her, wagging his tail as he always did when he greeted her in the morning.

"Hey, boy, it's still early, I'm going back to sleep again for a while." She moved to turn back over, but something caught her eye as she did. Pushing herself up on her elbows, she looked straight ahead at her doll's house, and there resting up against the wall of the house was an envelope that simply read, 'Faedra'.

She looked around the room, not quite sure what she expected to see, maybe her dad peeking through her door. Had he put it there as a surprise for her when she woke up? She got out of bed and wandered over to the doll's house, picked up the envelope and went back to sit under the covers. The envelope had an old-fashioned wax seal as a closure on the back.

"That's odd," she said, pulling her eyebrows together, "who on earth seals an envelope like that anymore?" She had seen plenty of examples of them in the museum, but never seen it on a modern day letter.

She opened the envelope with care, and pulled out a letter. She could feel something else in the envelope and tipped it up. A ring fell out onto her comforter. She picked it up so she could examine it.

"Wow, that's unusual," she whispered as she held the ring between her thumb and forefinger and inspected it from all angles. It looked very old. She didn't recognize the metal it was made from. It didn't look like gold or silver, although it did look gold in color, maybe some type of copper mix. There was no stone in the ring it was solid metal throughout. The main part of the ring was square, and had what looked like a Celtic design engraved on it. There was a different symbol in each of the four corners of the ring and they looked like little swirls going in different directions. The band came down from the square, and they too were engraved with several rows of etched lines. The band itself was thick. It was a ring of substance, but didn't look too oversized for a female to wear.

Faedra slid it on the ring finger of her right hand and it fit perfectly. As soon as the ring was in place a warm sensation emanated up her finger and throughout her hand. She stared at it, then brought her hand nearer to her face so she could inspect it more closely. Her eyes widened as she watched the symbols glow for a few seconds and then fade back to normal again.

She picked up the letter, and watched as goose bumps flashed up her arms, and an involuntary shiver was sent hurtling down her back. For some inexplicable reason she had a feeling that she was not going to like what this letter had to say, but after taking a deep steadying breath, she opened up the papers. She noticed that Faen was staring intently at her now as she scanned the top of the first page, which made her gasp.

"This is Mum's writing, I recognize it from my old birthday cards that I kept," she said to him, and then turned her attention back to the letter and started to read.

My Dearest Faedra,

If you are reading this letter, something prevented me from being with you on your 18th birthday and I have probably been taken from you and your father. There are things you need to know and it is best that you hear them from me. For that reason I wrote this letter to be given to you in the event that I could not be there in person. Before you read any further, make sure that you have Faen sitting beside you.

Faedra looked quizzically at her dog. "Mum says before I read this I need to have you beside me."

Faen pricked up his ears, jumped on the bed, laid his head on Faedra's leg, and looked at her. His beautiful amber eyes were burning with understanding.

"You *do* understand everything I say, don't you? And how does Mum know your name, you turned up after she had died?" She drew in a breath as the incomprehensible happenings of the recent past started to make the tiniest bit of sense, and continued to read the letter.

By now you may have been experiencing things that you cannot understand. I wish I were there to tell you myself and answer all your questions, of which I'm sure there will be plenty, but I shall start at the very beginning and hope that I can answer most.

Faedra, you are a direct descendant of an ancient Celtic bloodline. Thousands of years ago there was a family and they were fae. Yes faeries do exist. This family desperately wanted to become human and live in the World of Men. The fae king at the time could see their desire, although he could not understand it. They were so desperate that the king eventually granted them their wish, on one condition. Should he ever need their help in the World of Men, they would consent. The fae family agreed to his condition. In addition, the king allowed them each to keep one of their distinct powers, and more concerned for their well being than they seemed to be themselves, he also allowed them to keep their ability to heal much faster than normal humans.

The family lived happily among men for many years, and living among the fae had become a distant memory until one day the king visited them. He was seeking a place to secure a very precious element of fae heritage, and asked the family if they would look after it for him. Remembering the king's generosity and their previous agreement they agreed to his request, and he handed them the Amulet of Azran.

Let me explain a little more about the amulet. There is a book the fae use to help control nature, in all realms not just ours. It is a very powerful book called the Book of Anohs. The amulet was created to be utilized in conjunction with the book, and it has the power to control weather when the two elements are put together. On its own it is nothing more than a pretty trinket. The king realized that if the book and the amulet got into the wrong hands, the results could be devastating in all realms, and he was not willing to take that risk anymore.

You see there are two types of fae in Azran. There are the Light Fae, also known as the Seelie, who are good, and the Dark Fae, known as the Unseelie, who are evil. The king had reason to believe that the Unseelie were plotting to try and take control of the two elements. He bound the book with powerful magic to protect it, and hid the amulet in another realm... ours.

The amulet has been passed down throughout our descendants since it was given to them all those centuries ago. I was Custodian, but if you are reading this letter I have probably died and will have made sure that it was passed to you at the time of my death. You are now the Custodian of the Amulet of Azran.

Faedra looked up from the letter in disbelief, all kinds of crazy thoughts swimming around in her head.

"This is ridiculous, I'm a receptionist, the only thing I'm custodian of is the key to the coffee machine so I can refill the cups," she muttered to Faen then continued on with the letter.

First, we must get the amulet around your neck. Once you turn eighteen you must wear it always and never ever take it off. I cannot stress how important that is. It is warded so that only the Custodian can touch it. You will find the amulet in Arianne, the fairy I gave you. If you push her wings together they will unlock a secret compartment in the horse's body.

Faedra looked over to her fairies, eased herself out of bed, and crept over to her collection. She opened the glass door and plucked Arianne from the center of the shelf. She carried her back to bed and got back under the covers. Faedra sat and looked at Arianne for the longest time, staring at her in disbelief. Her heart was racing, and her hands started to tremble. She took a deep steadying breath and held the two outstretched wings between her thumb and forefinger, held her breath, and squeezed them together. The wings were stiff, and she was terrified of breaking them, but with a little more pressure they closed together, and Faedra heard a tiny click. She held Arianne around the waist and lifted her from the position she had, sitting astride the majestic black horse.

She peeked into the body of the horse. It was hollow, and inside was a small bundle of soft golden cloth. Reaching in with her fingers, she took hold of the small golden pouch and extracted it from its hiding place. She lay the horse down on the bed beside Arianne, and turned her attention to the pouch once more. Her fingers trembled again as she undid the thin gold braid that was tied around the top, and tipped it upside down allowing the contents to drop into the open palm of her other hand. She sucked in a deep breath.

The amulet was her mother's necklace. She had often wondered what happened to it, as she could not remember ever seeing her mother without it. But neither her nor her father had ever been able to find it after she died. Now she knew why, it had been hiding in her collection, in plain sight, for over a decade.

She had always loved this necklace, and stared down at it, not quite comprehending that she was holding it in her hand after all this time. The amulet triggered memories she had thought were forgotten, and they came flooding back to the forefront of her mind. Wonderful memories of the times she had spent with her mother.

The amulet was a pendant about an inch and a half in size, and triangular in shape. It looked like it was made of silver, and there were swirls covering the face of this piece too. *Celtic no doubt,* she thought. In the center was a beautiful yellow stone, which looked like a topaz. The facets of which sparkled in the sunlight that was spilling through the window.

Faedra gazed at the amulet for a few more moments, soaking up the memories it was provoking in her mind. She got up from the bed and walked over to her dresser, opened the clasp, and put the chain around her neck. As soon as the metal touched her skin the stone glowed, just for a second, but she definitely saw it glow in the reflection in the mirror. She wasn't sure of what she had seen when the ring had done it, thinking it was just a trick of the light. But this time she almost expected it, was waiting for it to do something. After a moment more of gazing at the amulet she got back on the bed, sat cross-legged on top of the comforter, and continued on with the letter.

The ring you found in the envelope is a Celtic battle ring. It is over two thousand years old, and was crafted by our ancestors. Wear it also, and never take it off. It will warn you if danger is near.

Now, here comes the tricky part.

Faedra raised her eyebrows at that comment. Her mother had thought that everything else she had explained so far in the letter was easy? She sighed, and continued reading.

Remember I said that we are descendants of an ancient fae family, and the members of this family were each allowed to keep one of their powers? You will have one; although no one knows which power they will inherit until they become of age. You are now of age, Faedra, and your power will grow to full strength shortly. You have probably also noticed by now that you heal incredibly quickly. This does not mean that you can't die or be killed you can, so be very very careful.

Until you turned of age you were protected by powerful wards that were put on you when you were born. Nothing evil could have penetrated those wards. Unfortunately, they dissipated the moment you turned eighteen and no longer protect you. Make it your duty to learn how to defend yourself. Hopefully, you will not have a need to use defensive measures, as only three people know the whereabouts of the amulet. Faen will be able to teach you all you need to know.

Now, that brings me to the subject of Faen.

Faedra looked at her dog, who was still sitting on the bed watching her intently.

I have explained about as much as I can in a letter and I will leave the rest to Faen. I asked the day you were born that he be assigned as your Guardian if anything should happen to me. It is probably easier if Faen shows you, rather than me try to explain it. Please do not be afraid, he will look after you. Now, if I could ask you to say out loud the phrase at the bottom of this letter.

I love you my darling, take care and learn all you can.

Forever, Mum

Faedra's goose bumps returned with a vengeance, and she looked up from the letter to stare at her dog who was now sitting up attentively, watching and waiting. She looked down at the letter again, and back at Faen. She did this several times, her mind whirling, confusion splashed all over her face. Finally she took a deep breath, looked down at the letter, and read with a quiver in her voice.

"Faen, please show yourself?" It came out more like a question than a statement.

Faen jumped off the bed and stood in front of her on the floor. What happened next was a bit of a blur; actually that's exactly what happened. Her dog blurred, and a split second later, in its place stood a man.

She threw her hand up to cover her mouth as a scream broke free from her vocal chords. She knew if her dad heard he would be up the stairs and through her door in a flash. She backed herself up against the headboard, and stared with wide frightened eyes at the stranger standing just a few feet away. Her heart pounded so hard all she could hear was the pulse in her ears. Her hands went clammy, and her breathing quickened.

"Do not be alarmed, Ms. Bennett," Faen's voice was calm and steady. "I will not harm you."

Faedra couldn't speak, her throat had closed up. She could see the concern spreading across the man's face, and he started to move towards her with his hand outstretched. She edged herself along the bed, pushing the bed covers away with her feet as they scrambled to push her back further until she was nearly at the other edge of the bed. The man acknowledged her fear and stepped back. She stopped moving when he did, and took a breath. He took another step back and stood quietly, sensing that he would have to let Faedra try and get her head around what was happening before he could continue. It wasn't an every day occurrence to have a strange man materialize in her bedroom. He should know, he had been there every day for the past eleven years.

A few moments passed in silence. Faedra did not take her eyes off the man who was now standing motionless in the corner of her room. He returned her gaze, not taking his eyes from hers either. As the sudden shock slowly abated, her heartbeat calmed, and her breathing returned to normal. She regained some composure and sat up straighter on her bed instead of embedding herself into the headboard. Cautiously, she released the hand from her mouth, and for the first time, took in the features of the man who was standing in the exact same spot where her dog had been just a couple of minutes before.

He was beautiful. From head to toe everything about him was perfect, fairy-tale perfect. He didn't look much older than her, maybe twenty. He had blonde hair that looked like pure silk, and she watched as he ran his hand through it, was he nervous too perhaps? His aqua blue eyes shone with a brightness that held her captive. He had a strong jaw and chiseled cheekbones, and stood about six feet tall. To be honest he looked like he'd stepped straight out of an animated Disney movie, especially dressed as he was.

He wore knee high brown leather boots that turned over with a cuff at the top, light brown leather breeches that hugged the contours of his legs to perfection. A cream loose fitting tunic-style shirt with long puffy sleeves made of thin cotton, and edged with gold trim that skimmed the top of his thighs. The tunic had a v-shaped neckline that showed a hint of his muscular chest, and an ancient looking Celtic talisman hung from a black leather thong around his neck. An impressive sword hung from a leather belt at his waist, prompting Faedra to fleetingly wonder if the artists at Disney were, in fact, fairies themselves.

She blinked several times and shook the thought away to return to the matter at hand.

"Wh-who *are* you?" Faedra stuttered.

"My name is Faen, Ms. Bennett."

"But that's my dog's name. Faen is your real name?"

"It is. Pray tell me, you could have called me anything, where did you think of the name Faen?"

Faedra narrowed her eyes at him, searching in her mind for the memory.

"I-I, my mother," she remembered. "I overheard my mum mention your name once and it stuck with me. You knew her too?"

"I did."

"You turned up the day of my mum's funeral. I was sitting on my swing crying. I wrapped my arms around your neck, and you let me hug you for ages. I remember, my dad didn't have the heart to shoo you away, and he let me keep you as a pet, but all this time you were sent here to what? Protect me?"

"Yes."

"What are you?"

"I am Fae, Ms. Bennett."

"That's a fairy, right?"

"You are correct, Ms. Bennett," he replied with an incline of his head.

Faedra let out a sigh. "Stop calling me that. You make me sound like a character out of a Jane Austin novel."

Faen frowned. "I do not understand, that is your name, is it not?"

"No, I mean yes it is, but it sounds so… formal."

"Ms. Bennett, as a Guardian I am taught to treat my charge with the utmost respect."

"Please, Faen," she pleaded. "Call me Faedra."

"Very well, as you wish, Ms. Faedra."

Faedra raised her eyes heavenward, she could sense he was not going to compromise any more than that.

"Great, now you make me sound like a school teacher," she whispered under her breath.

She looked at him thoughtfully for a moment, something having just occurred to her. She was sensing no danger from the stranger in her room, so she eased herself off the bed, and moved towards him. He did not move, but just continued to watch her.

"May I ask you a personal question?" she asked as she meandered around him, looking intently at his back. Faen followed her with his eyes as far as he could, but continued to stand very still.

"Of course."

"Aren't fairies supposed to have wings? You don't have any wings."

"I have wings, Ms. Faedra. I choose not to show them," he replied with what Faedra thought was a look of discomfort, embarrassment even.

"Why?"

"I have my reasons," he responded with just a hint of sharpness that cut through his otherwise silken voice.

Again Faedra sensed that was as much as he was going to say on the subject.

"So let me get this straight, you can change from a fairy into a dog?"

"Most fae have the ability to shape shift into an animal, though not necessarily one of our choosing, and as you can see," he waved a hand down the length of his body, "we tend to stick with the same coloring in both our forms."

Faedra walked around to face him, and studied his beautiful features. They were very hard not to stare at. Then something else occurred to her, and her eyes widened with horror as what she was thinking sank in. She ran over to her bed, sat on the end of it, and buried her head in her hands to hide her crimson cheeks.

"Oh NO!" she groaned.

Faen moved then, he moved with impossible swiftness, and was kneeling in front of her at the foot of the bed in the blink of an eye, unable to hide his look of concern.

"Ms. Faedra, what is wrong?" he asked softly.

"This can't be happening," she repeated into her hands.

"Ms. Faedra, please tell me. I can help."

"All these years," she continued.

"All these years what, Ms. Faedra? Please, talk to me," Faen was almost pleading with her. Faedra kept her face buried securely in her hands.

"Ms. Faedra, please look at me," he whispered. "Tell me what is wrong."

A moment passed, and Faedra didn't move. Faen reached up tentatively to touch her hands. He took hold of them, and pulled them away from her face. Her eyes were tightly closed, her cheeks still beet red.

"Please, look at me," he asked again. She opened her eyes and looked deeply into his. He could see embarrassment and confusion warring in her expression. "Whatever is the matter?"

Faedra swallowed hard. "All this time, I thought you were a dog."

"Yes," he said, willing her to go on.

"I can't even begin to imagine how many times," she paused, "I have got undressed in front of you," her voice quivered.

Faen looked at her with a confused expression at first, then slowly the realization of what she had just told him started to sink in. "Oh, Ms. Faedra, I assure you that I always looked away any time that you were, um how shall I say, not decent."

"Really?"

"Really."

Faedra exhaled, she hadn't realized she'd been holding her breath all this time. She smiled down at Faen, and he smiled back at her. It almost took her breath away how his smile lit up his face. It was the first time he had smiled at her in this form. When she thought about it a bit more she could remember noticing that her dog always turned away from her when she was getting undressed. She'd never paid it much attention before, but it made perfect sense now.

"Are you sure you never peeked, not even once?"

Faen's eyes widened with alarm at her question. "No, Ms. Faedra, never. I swear to you."

She studied his face and decided she believed him, and let out a giggle. "Phew."

"Although the impromptu hairbrush concerts were always entertaining," he said, his lips curling into a wry smile.

Her shoulders slumped, and her cheeks flushed again as she recalled the endless times she had danced around her room. Singing at the top of her lungs into her hairbrush to whatever was playing in the CD player at the time. She bopped him on the arm, it was a spontaneous reaction.

"Faedra," her dad called from the top of her stairs a split second before he knocked on her door. She turned her head sharply in the direction of the door then turned back to Faen. He was sitting in front of her wagging his tail.

"That was quick," she whispered to him then narrowed her eyes. "Where on earth do you put that sword?"

"Faedra?" her dad asked again.

She looked behind her and threw the bed covers over the letter, and her dismantled figurine.

"Come in, Dad," she answered.

The door opened and her dad walked in carrying a tray with a cup of tea and a present on it.

"Happy Birthday, darling," he announced, beamed a big grin at her. She got up and walked over to give him a kiss.

"Thanks, Dad."

CHAPTER SIX

"You didn't have to bring me tea, Dad, I would have been down in a minute," she told her father, knowing full well she had forgotten all parameters of time, as well as the fact it was her birthday.

"If I can't spoil my only daughter on her birthday, I'm not much of a father now am I? I've made you bacon and eggs, too." He smiled, and then froze as his eyes caught sight of the amulet hanging from her neck.

Faedra felt her stomach knot. It hadn't even occurred to her that she would have to explain where she had gotten her mother's necklace from, especially since they both had been searching for it for the past eleven years.

"Your mother's necklace," he exclaimed. "Where did you get it?"

"What, you didn't leave it for me?" she asked, thinking quickly on her feet.

"Me? No," he replied, narrowing his eyes at her.

"Well it was hanging on the chimney stack of my doll's house this morning, along with this ring, and she held her hand out for him to see. I thought you had sneaked up last night and put them there as a surprise."

Please fall for it, she thought desperately. It was the only story she could think of, he had to fall for it.

"Well that's just plain odd," he raised his eyebrows. "I've never believed in ghosts, but you know, Fae, every now and then I sense something quite odd in this house. Maybe your mum put them there."

Faedra inwardly released a sigh of relief. *That was close.*

"Could be," she agreed, with just a little too much enthusiasm.

"Well come on, let's go and have some breakfast before it goes cold, I even cooked some up for Faen, too."

She looked over at Faen and winked, a knowing smile curving her lips. Faen's ear had pricked up at the sound of the word bacon.

"Come on, Boy," she cringed at her words. A boy he most certainly was not.

Henry still had hold of the tray, and turned to carry it back down the stairs, followed closely by Faedra and Faen.

"Not quite sure why I brought this up to you," he muttered. "Just thought it would be a nice gesture."

"It was a wonderful gesture, Dad, thanks."

They wandered into the kitchen, and Faedra's heart swelled.

"Oh, Dad, you didn't have to go to all this trouble."

He put the tray down on the table and she wrapped her arms around him to give him a big hug. Laid out across the table were plates of scrambled eggs, bacon, toast, and pancakes. All of her favorite breakfast foods were there. She noticed three plates set out on the table, and she looked with curiosity at her father.

"I told you one was for Faen," he answered her questioning look, leaned over to pick the plate off the table and lay it on the floor in front of his daughter's shaggy white dog.

The newly appointed Custodian couldn't help herself, she giggled. The image of the beautiful prince-like fairy that was in her room just a few minutes before, and was now eating off a plate on the floor, was just too ironic. She didn't know whether to laugh or cry, and decided laughing was the better option.

"What's so funny, young lady?" her dad asked, a bemused expression creeping across his face.

"You wouldn't believe me if I told you," she said with a sigh. Faedra could hardly believe it herself. Looking down at her beloved dog, she wondered whether it had all just been a daydream.

They sat at the table and tucked into the breakfast that her father had lovingly prepared for her birthday. Today was a going to be a very unusual day, of that she had no doubt.

"Open your present," her dad said, passing her the colorfully wrapped gift.

She took it, and opened the wrapping with care. She had always hated to tear the paper and wondered why; it wasn't as if she was likely to use it again. Inside was a square velvet box. She opened it and gasped.

"Oh, Dad, it's beautiful. You shouldn't have." She picked up the bracelet and gave it a closer look. It was a silver bangle, which had a Celtic design that ran the whole circumference of it. "Thank you. I'll wear it always." *Along with the Battle ring and the Amulet of Azran.* She was getting quite a collection of Celtic jewelry given to her that day.

"You're welcome sweetheart, I'm glad you like it. So what are your plans for today?" her dad asked.

She finished her mouthful before she answered. Her mum had always taught her it was rude to talk with your mouth full of food.

Well, I was going to go shopping with Amy and Zoë, and buy an outfit for going out this evening, like any normal eighteen year old on her birthday. But I found out I'm the Custodian to an ancient fae amulet, and my dog turned into a fairy, so I have a feeling those plans are going to be cancelled. She was relieved her dad couldn't read minds.

"Haven't really thought about it, I'll probably go and take Gypsy out for a ride," she answered him with a smile. She needed more time alone with Faen. She hadn't anywhere near had all her questions answered yet. They were piling up so fast she thought her head might explode if she didn't get them out soon.

"Well as long as you've got something planned and you're not going to be spending the day alone."

How ironic, she thought, *I'm never going to be spending the day alone again.*

"Your Uncle Leo asked me to go and help him with something, so I hope you don't mind, but I'll be gone most of the day," Henry continued, pulling Faedra from deep inside her thoughts.

"Huh? Oh no problem, Dad, that's fine, I'll have plenty to do."

"Good, well I'll just go and let your uncle know I'll be there in a little while." Henry got up from the table to go and use the phone.

"*You* have got a lot more explaining to do," she told Faen as soon as her dad was out of earshot. Faen's ears drooped, and he raised a furry eyebrow.

When her dad returned to the table they finished their breakfast, and she helped him clear up and load the dishwasher.

"I'm off now then, darling," Henry announced, and leaned down to kiss his daughter on the forehead. "I'll see you later."

"Okay, Dad, have fun with Uncle Leo, tell him hello from me, and I'll see him and Nicki soon."

"Will do, bye then." Henry disappeared around the corner, and she heard the door close behind him.

She looked at Faen who was still in his dog form, and shook her head. Maybe it was all a daydream. She got up, and padded through the dining room and up the stairs to her bedroom, followed by her faithful companion. When she reached the top of the stairs she opened her door, and turned to look at him.

"Oh no you don't, you're staying right here, I'm going to get dressed." And closed the door behind her, leaving him sitting on the top stair.

She rested back against the closed door for a moment, looked at the messy covers strewn all over her bed, and blew out a long breath.

"I have a feeling my world has just been turned upside down," she mumbled to herself as she wandered over to the bed to straighten it out. She picked up Arianne and the horse, and slotted them back together, taking care not to break them, and replaced the reassembled figurine in the cabinet. She picked up the letter, folded it, and placed it back in its envelope, then slid it under some other papers that were inside her nightstand. She would figure out what to do with that later. She was sure she would have to read it over several times more before everything sunk in.

There was a scratch at the door.

"You're not coming in, Faen, and that's final. I'll be out in a minute."

She wandered over to her closet and turned to look out the window. It looked like it was going to be a warm, sunny summer's day, and she chose a t-shirt and shorts, throwing them on quickly. She had to admit to herself, she could not bear to be parted from her dog for very long, and was itching to have some more questions answered.

When she opened her door, she was startled and took a step back. She was expecting to see furry Faen sitting there waiting, but it was Faen in his true form. He was standing, waiting for her in the doorway, and had a very imposing presence that took her by surprise.

"This is going to take a bit of getting used to," she told him.

"I apologize, Ms. Faedra, I startled you. That was not my intention."

"No worries. So what now?" she asked. She was not quite sure how to continue from here.

"Our priority is to find out what your power is, and how to control it," he said very matter-of-factly, as if it was the most normal thing in the world to inherit a power on your eighteenth birthday. "And I believe that would be better done outside. Things have a tendency to get broken upon initial attempts."

He stood to the side, and gestured for her to pass. She did, and walked down the stairs, and they headed outside.

It was a beautiful day, the sun was shining and it was pleasantly balmy.

Faen sat down in the shade of an impressive oak tree that still had a swing hanging from a large bough. The same swing Faedra had sat on when they first met eleven years ago. She took the same spot now, letting her legs dangle freely in the warm breeze. Faen leaned his back up against the gnarly trunk and focused his attention on her.

She was looking at him a little differently now. She was not so dumbstruck by his beauty, but was more contemplating the fact that he was even there at all. She couldn't help but keep looking around expecting her dog to be right next to her, and a strange feeling of loss crept like tendrils around her heart. She would never be able to have the same relationship with her dog again. He would now, and forever be, this incredible man that was sitting before her, even when he was in his dog form.

Faen could see that she was trying to digest the information she had received so far this morning, and was not sure how much more she could handle in one day. He knew she was strong. Had spent eleven years watching her grow from strength to strength, but he had also seen her vulnerable side, and he didn't want to push her too far. So they sat in silence for a while, he would let her talk first when she was ready. He would be patient, and he had all the patience in the world for the precious young girl he had watched grow up into a beautiful young lady.

It had sounded like Henry was going to be out for most of the day, so there was plenty of time before she was due to go out with her friends this evening.

Faedra drew in a breath, as though she were getting ready to say something, thought better of it, and exhaled again. A few moments passed and she did the same thing. She was itching to know what those eyes had belonged to in the woods, and at the graveyard, but knew she would not like the answer, and was putting off the inevitable.

Finally she bit the bullet. "What were those things in the woods and at the graveyard?" she asked.

"Redcaps," he replied.

"What are Redcaps?"

"They are Unseelie, evil and murderous. There are not many Unseelie left, but the few that remain usually wreak havoc in realms other than Azran, since the King has tried to wipe them out. They can be mercenary, and will hire themselves out if the prize is right. Do not worry, you were warded, and they could not have hurt you. Myself and Jocelyn just did not want them to get anywhere near you. Their features would certainly have frightened you."

"But I'm not warded anymore," she stated as she started scanning the perimeter of her garden with growing concern.

"You are safe here, Ms. Faedra. Your house and grounds have been warded for centuries, nothing can get past the property boundaries if it has evil intent," he continued.

"But I can't stay in here forever, I'm going out with my friends tonight to celebrate my birthday. What do they want with me anyway and how did they find me? It said in Mum's letter that only three people know the whereabouts of the amulet, and only two of them know about me."

Faen's face mirrored the look of concern that Faedra was feeling. "I do not know what they want, or how they found you. You, the King of Azran, and myself are the only ones who are supposed to have knowledge of the amulet. The King, and myself, the only ones who know about you."

"Forgive me for not sounding very confident in that, when some murderous evil fairies have been coming after me, before *I* even know who I am."

"I will teach you to defend yourself, Ms. Faedra, and I will not leave your side again," he said, trying to reassure her.

She hung her head, not wanting to ask the next question, but needing to know. "My mum didn't die of a mysterious illness did she?" She looked over and studied his features. Her heart ached when she saw the sorrow and regret on his face.

"No," he replied, "she did not." His eyes reflected his sadness as he remembered lifting Lillith's battered body from the hard cold gravel pathway behind the church. She had put up a good fight but had been overpowered, and instead of killing her swiftly, the Redcaps had poisoned her. Leaving her to die a slow painful death. He didn't understand why. They were usually so swift with their killings, which only led him to believe that they were doing someone else's bidding. As yet, he had not discovered for whom that was. Because of the speed with which she healed, Lillith's bruises had almost disappeared by the time he had gotten her home. So her husband and daughter were left wondering what had made her so sick, and why it had happened so suddenly.

"Were you her Guardian too? Weren't you supposed to protect her?" Faedra's voice took on a demanding tone.

"Yes, Ms. Faedra, on both counts."

"Well you didn't do a very good job did you?" Faedra snapped. Her voice was laced with the bitterness she had carried for so long because of losing her mother at such an early age.

Faen's face fell, and he hung his head. "Your mother sent me to run an errand, I should not have left her, but she insisted. I will be eternally remorseful for my actions that day," he looked up and shot a determined glare at Faedra. "You can be sure, Ms. Faedra, I will not make the same mistake twice."

Faedra averted her eyes from his. She felt a little ashamed of her outburst. Being mean was not a natural occurrence for her, but she had never had anyone or anything to blame for her mother's death before, and the feeling of needing to place blame was suddenly overwhelming.

"I'm sorry, I didn't mean to sound, well, you know," she spoke softly again.

"Do not concern yourself, it was no more than I deserved. Your mother was a wonderful, caring person. She was a very talented Custodian, and could fight like no human I had ever seen before. Her sword skills were beyond measure."

Faedra shook her head. "My mum knew how to fight? With a sword?"

"Yes, the best I have ever seen in a human."

"Whoa," she breathed.

"She should have been the one to teach you, but she had found out something, and was on her way to tell the King. She was intercepted before she got to the portal."

"So you're telling me my mum was… murdered?"

Faen hung his head again, averting his gaze. "Yes, Ms. Faedra, she was."

In an instant the need to blame someone was fiercely overshadowed with a need for revenge. A feeling that shook Faedra to the core. She had never felt such a strong emotion before, and it scared her. She slid down from the swing and stood in front of Faen with her hands, that were balled into fists, resting on her hips.

"Show me!" she demanded. "You tell me I have a power. Show me how to find it and use it."

Faen looked up at the determined young lady who was standing over him. Her eyes flashed with a passion he had never witnessed in her before, a passion for revenge. He rose in one fluid movement, and in the blink of an eye was standing right in front of her, inches from her face. She blinked back her surprise at the swiftness with which he could move, but held her position and did not flinch or step back.

That's a promising start, he thought, *she stood her ground. Moving like that would make most humans jump out of their skin.* He held her gaze steady with his. In another blink of an eye he was behind her, but somehow she had anticipated the move and had turned immediately, and was facing him again. Her eyes flashed with anger this time.

He rubbed his chin. *Lightening reflexes, another good sign.*

He wanted to try something else, just to test his theory on her reflexes, and made to grab her by the throat. Instantaneously she ducked, avoiding his grip and kicked his legs out from under him, but instead of falling to the ground, he just hovered on his side in mid air as if he were relaxing on an invisible platform. Propping himself up on his elbow, he gave her a wry smile.

She scowled at him. "What are you doing?" she snapped. "Stop messing about and start teaching me how to defend myself." Then she thought for a moment about what she had just done.

"Ms. Faedra, I think you are going to be a natural at this, just like your mother." He smiled as he lowered his feet to the ground, and stood up again.

She considered her reaction for a moment. It had all happened so fast she hadn't even thought about it. "How did I do that?" she asked.

"As I said, you are going to be a natural at this," he repeated. "Now let us begin trying to discover what power you hold. I have observed you blowing on your hands repeatedly over the past few weeks. Your power could be connected with them."

"Of course, that would make sense. Thank Goodness I'm not going mad, although I have to wonder if this is all a dream, and I'm going to wake up any second."

"Be assured, Ms. Faedra, it is not a dream. Now concentrate on your hands and see if you can feel anything unusual," he instructed.

She looked at her hands and channeled all her thoughts to them. Nothing happened, not even the slightest tingle.

"Nothing happened," she said in dismay.

"Try again," he instructed, circling her now.

She closed her eyes this time and concentrated hard. Still nothing.

"Try again," Faen repeated.

She did, and again and again for about an hour, but still nothing.

"I need to take a break," she whispered.

"Try again," Faen insisted.

"No. I need a break."

"The Redcaps will not give you a break, Ms. Faedra. Try again."

She squared her shoulders at him, and held her hands out for him to see. "Well, I must be broken then because it's not working. I obviously don't have this so called power."

"Yes you do. Try again," he was incessant.

Frustration was starting to get the better of her.

"Faen, I do not have any powers!" she shouted as she flicked her hands out in defeat. Her eyes widened in utter disbelief as she watched two balls of light shoot from her palms and were on a collision course with Faen's head. He twisted his torso with lightening speed and the balls flew past him, narrowly missing his ear, and exploded against the tree trunk leaving scorch marks in the bark. She closed her hands and held them to her chest.

"Careful, Ms. Faedra, you nearly took my ear off," he said with a smile. He looked at her with the proud admiration of a parent whose child had just received an A in math.

"Sorry," she squeaked.

"Oh do not be. That was very impressive for your first time," he praised. "This is very advantageous. You can control energy, electrical energy it would seem. Humans are made up of electrical impulses, and your power gives you the ability to mold that energy and send it outside of your body.

When you have had more practice you will be able to mold outside sources of energy too."

She gawped at him, it was all she could do. She hadn't woken up from any dream yet, so she had to try and accept the fact that she had just flung two balls of light across the yard and nearly blew up the tree.

"Can you remember what you were feeling when your power materialized?" he asked. "Could you try and reenact that again, but with a little more control this time?"

She could remember, she felt anger and frustration.

"I'll Try." She closed her eyes holding her palms up, and imagined her mum being attacked by the Redcaps. Anger seared through her, and she opened her eyes in shock when she realized it wasn't the anger that seared her, it was the energy she was sending from all over her body into the palms of her hands. She stared at the balls of light that she had created that were now bobbing above each of her palms.

"Very good, Ms. Faedra," Faen smiled.

She looked up at him and smiled back. The balls of light fizzled out and disappeared. This power seemed to be connected to negative emotion and that wasn't something she was used to feeling. She didn't like the idea that she would have to make herself angry or frustrated to be able to use it.

"Faen?" She asked. "I don't want to have to be angry to conjure my power. I don't like feeling that way."

"Do not worry, this is just the beginning, you will learn to control your power much more easily as time progresses. At present, heightened emotion enables you to pull your power forward. In time you will learn to control it without negative emotion. Although, it will always be strongest when your feelings are running high. That is just the natural order of things. Not much different to the 'fight or flight' response humans have to danger. It will be most powerful when the need for it is greatest."

They decided to take a break for a while and Faedra lifted herself back up onto the swing, and watched as Faen lowered himself to the ground to lean against the oak tree.

"What power did my mother have?" she asked.

"Your mother was telekinetic, she could move things with her mind."

His reply sparked a memory that Faedra had almost forgotten, but in a flash it was there again, clear as day. She had walked into the dining room one morning when she was little. Her mother was doing some dusting, and humming to herself. She had had her back to Faedra and hadn't heard her walk in. She was standing on a chair reaching up to try and dust the light hanging from the tall ceiling, but couldn't quite reach it, so she opened her hands and the duster floated up to the light, and started dusting by itself. Faedra had let out a gasp causing her mother to turn to look at her, and the duster had fallen gracefully to the floor. Lillith had flushed, picked up the duster and gone about her business as if nothing had happened, and Faedra had never been able to quite believe what she had seen, so put it to the darkest recesses of her mind.

She thought of something else, too. She was going to ask the question when Faen had mentioned it, but got caught up in another thought, and had forgotten about it until now.

"Faen, you mentioned earlier that you and Jocelyn were keeping the Redcaps away from me. Who is Jocelyn?"

He sighed. "She is my little sister."

Faedra's eyebrows shot up. "You have a little sister?"

"Yes, I do," he replied stoically. "She is the black and white dog you see at the church. She guards the portal to the Land of Azran."

Could sibling love and rivalry be the same for fairies as for humans, she wondered. Faedra laughed, and Faen narrowed his eyes at her. "Well that growling thing you do with her makes perfect sense now," she responded to his frown. "My friend's little brother gets on her nerves all the time, but she still loves him, even if she can't stand him sometimes."

He didn't respond.

"Wait, you said she guards the portal. There's a portal at the church?"

"Yes."

"Wow, we can get to your world at the church?"

"Yes."

"So how come the vicar couldn't see her that day when I asked him if she was his?"

"She used glamour to hide herself."

"Ooh," Faedra shuffled excitedly on the swing, her eyes sparkling with enthusiasm. "I know what that means, it means you can choose to make other people see what you want them to see, doesn't it? I remember that from an episode of *Charmed*."

Faen gave her a martyred look, he remembered that episode of Charmed also. Along with all the others in the seven seasons he had watched with her. It was her favorite show, and she had never missed a single one.

Faedra practiced using her power for several more hours, watched by Faen as he relaxed against the ancient oak tree. He was impressed by how swiftly she was becoming adept at focusing her thoughts and creating balls of light in her palms, but she had not yet mastered, apart from that very first time, the art of being able to throw them at a target. They dissipated into sparks just a few inches from her hands, and he could tell she was getting tired. It was, after all, her energy she was throwing away each time, and she had to replenish it with something to eat or she would get weak very quickly.

"I think you have had enough for one day, Ms. Faedra," he said as he rose in that fluid motion of his and was, in the blink of an eye, standing before her. "You need to eat, you are growing tired. Remember, this is your energy you are expelling. You need to replenish it often."

"Just one more try?" she asked.

He didn't answer. Before she even had time to comprehend it, he was gone, and her dog was sitting in front of her. She heard a noise and looked up to see her dad's car coming down the driveway.

CHAPTER SEVEN

Faedra and Faen strolled over to where her dad had parked his car, and greeted him as he opened the car door.

"Hi, Dad, did you have a nice time with Uncle Leo?" she asked.

"Actually, we had a very nice time," he replied with a smile as he got out of the car, and planted a kiss on his daughter's forehead, "how about you, did you go for a ride on Gyspy?"

She had forgotten all about her horse, and the ride she was supposed to take that day.

"No I didn't in the end," she said, playing for time until she could come up with an excuse as to why she hadn't. "I just ended up relaxing in the garden. I didn't want to wear myself out and be tired this evening."

He gave her a thoughtful look. "Well I'm not sure how much relaxing you did, Darling, you look exhausted."

"Do I?" She feigned ignorance and made up another excuse. Truth was, she did feel exhausted after using up all that energy practicing with her power for most of the day. "I'm just hungry, I was going in to get myself a sandwich when you drove up."

They all headed to the front door. Henry opened it and gestured for Faedra and Faen to enter first.

"What time are your friends picking you up this evening?"

"They're coming round about seven."

"I know I haven't really mentioned this before because you are always so sensible but I feel, as your father, I need to say something."

Faedra smiled, she had been expecting the 'I know you are legally old enough to drink but don't over do it' speech. "Don't worry, Dad, Amy is designated driver tonight, and I promise I'll only have a couple. I have no intention of waking up with a throbbing headache tomorrow morning."

Henry looked visibly relieved by her response.

Faedra wandered through the dining room towards the kitchen to make herself a sandwich, and caught a sideways glance of her reflection in the mirror hanging on one of the walls as she walked past. She stopped dead and reversed back a few steps until she was standing in front of it, and looked with surprise at the person staring back at her with a shocked expression.

"Oh my God, I'm nearly gray," she gasped as she took in her features. Her skin had taken on a pallid grayish tinge and there were dark circles developing under her eyes. "No wonder dad thought I looked exhausted. I look like I've got one foot in the grave."

She rushed into the kitchen and made herself a plate of sandwiches, wolfing them down with lightening speed.

"Steady on," Henry said as he walked through the door and caught Faedra stuffing a whole sandwich in her mouth, giving her chipmunk cheeks. "You'll get indigestion if you eat that quickly. Anyway, wanted to let you know that I'm going out with your uncle tonight, so I'll be leaving around six thirty."

She acknowledged him with a nod of her head, her mouth still full to overflowing with the sandwich she had just stuffed in there. She looked over at the clock on the oven. She had a couple more hours to go before her friends arrived, that should give her plenty of time to get ready, and hopefully to re-energize. She certainly didn't want to go out looking like she was on her last leg, and prayed that the sandwiches would do the trick.

They did, a half hour later she dared herself to look in the mirror again, and her usually radiant skin and sparkling eyes stared back at her. She heaved a huge sigh of relief and made a mental note to take snack breaks while practicing with her power in the future.

She went to her room, grabbed her bathrobe, and made her way to the bathroom to take a shower and get ready for her evening out with friends. She was looking forward to it. When she had finished with her shower she wandered back to her room, her hair piled on top of her head, wrapped in a towel. Faen had waited patiently outside the bathroom, and was following her up the stairs to her bedroom. When they got to the top of the stairs he lay down and didn't attempt to enter her room this time.

"Thank you," she whispered as she closed the door.

She padded over to her dresser and commenced her ritual of putting make up on and drying her hair. The former didn't take long at all, she had almost perfect skin, so just a dusting of powder, a little eye shadow, mascara, and lip-gloss, and she was done. The latter took considerably more time, as her hair was so long and thick. She turned her head upside down and continued on with the arduous task.

A while later when her hair was dried and styled, her face glowing, and natural, she wandered over to her closet. Due to the fact that she hadn't done what most teenage girls do on their eighteenth birthday and go shopping for a new outfit, she looked with deliberation at the clothes that already existed there, and decided on a pretty royal blue dress with thin straps. It had a fitted bodice that nipped neatly in at the waist flowing into a full skirt that skimmed her hips, accentuating her figure perfectly. The color complimented her skin and hair, and she felt really good in it.

"I'm off now, Fae," she heard her dad call from the bottom of the stairs.

"Okay, Dad, have fun tonight."

"You, too, darling. Hey, did you know Faen was out here?" he asked in surprise.

"Yes, Dad, I'll let him in a minute."

She heard her dad mutter something about never knowing Faen to be shut out of her room before, as he walked out of the dining room.

She sighed, she had to admit it did feel kind of odd not having him in with her, but that dynamic had completely changed now, and would never be the same again. There was a heavy feeling in her heart at the thought. Her dad's car door slammed, and she watched from her window as he drove up the driveway and out of sight.

She wandered back to the closet and took one last look at her reflection in the full-length mirror that was attached to one of the doors. That'll do, she thought with a smile and wandered over to her door to let Faen in. She never knew which form he would be in now, but guessed that because her father had left he would probably be in his true form.

She was right. Faen was standing in her doorway when she opened it, all six feet of him. He didn't make her jump this time and she looked up at his face, and smiled. She wasn't sure, but as his eyes skimmed over her, his usually stoic features melted for just a split second to reveal something more like warm approval, but then it was gone in an instant. She wondered why he was so loving with her when he was in his dog form. Always wagging his tail, always looking pleased to see her. But in his true form he seemed distant, almost as though being there was an inconvenience. She brushed the thought aside. It seemed like they were stuck together for the time being, whether either of them wanted to be or not. At the very least, until she had learned all she could to defend herself against the Unseelie.

"You look very nice, Ms. Faedra," he broke the silence, and pulled her from her reverie.

"Thank you."

"Where are you going tonight?" he asked.

"The Old Brewery House in the village," she narrowed her eyes at him. "Why?"

"Because I am going with you, of course," he replied.

"Oh, I don't think so," she said defiantly. "It's a girl's night out with my friends, you can't come."

"I will be there whether you like it or not," he reiterated with a firmness that was undeniable. "I told you, I will not make the same mistake twice. Do not concern yourself, I will blend into the background, no one else will have to know I am there."

She looked him up and down. Blending into the background was not something Faen would accomplish, dressed as he was.

She sighed. "Okay, I understand that you want to stay close to me, but you will definitely not blend in dressed like that." And she gestured down his body with her hand as if showcasing something unusual.

He looked himself up and down, and returned his gaze to her. "What's wrong with what I am wearing?" he asked.

"You look like you have walked straight out of a Disney movie," she replied somewhat sarcastically, then kicked herself for sounding so rude.

He looked perplexed.

"Faen, what you are wearing is very old fashioned, you have seen how humans dress nowadays. You need to wear something more… modern.

"Oh, modern," he replied. "I can do modern." And with one of his blurs he was standing in front of her in a complete change of clothes.

She took a step back, and sucked in a breath. She hadn't expected him to look so good in modern clothing.

"Ms. Faedra, you look shocked are you alright."

"Absolutely fine," she squeaked, as she took in the ultra modern Faen.

From top to toe he was dressed in designer clothing. Shiny black boots with a square toe. Jeans that were belted at his waist with a black leather belt, accentuated with a buckle that looked like a silver Celtic rose. He wore a black t-shirt that fit him like a glove, skimming every contour of his torso and upper arms. She swallowed hard, it was an involuntary response.

"Will this work?" he asked.

"Yes," she breathed, "that will work just fine." Then she noticed the design on his belt buckle and lifted her wrist to examine the bangle her father had given her earlier.

"Your buckle, it's the same design as my bracelet."

Faen looked at her and the corners of his mouth turned up very slightly in a knowing smile.

"You did that on purpose, didn't you?"

She was distracted by the crunch of gravel as a car appeared coming down the driveway. When she turned back to him he was holding a tiny clay pot with a cork stopper in the palm of his hand.

"You will need this," he said, offering her the pot.

"What is it?"

"Rub a little on your eyelids, you will be able to see all fae now, even if they are trying to hide themselves with glamour."

She did as instructed and rubbed some of the ointment over her eyelids. She figured she could use all the help she could get. A warm buzz lingered on her eyelids for a second, but when she opened her eyes and looked around, nothing seemed out of the ordinary.

"Thank you."

Faen nodded a 'you're welcome.' Then they both turned their heads when a loud rapping could be heard from the front door.

"That will be Amy and Zoë, stay here until I'm gone, you know where the Old Brewery is. I'll see you there," she made to leave, and then thought of something else. "Oh, and Faen, please try to look inconspicuous."

"I will try, Ms. Faedra."

She grabbed her purse and almost ran down the stairs. Faen watched from the window as Faedra got in the back of her friend's car. As soon as they were out of sight he was outside. Although the pub was a few minutes down the road by car, he arrived before they did.

***

"Good grief the car park is full tonight," Faedra commented as they pulled in.

"It's Saturday, Fae, what do you expect?" Zoë replied.

They got out, and looked up at the outside of the pub. Actually, it was more than just a pub. It was a Georgian house that had been built in the late eighteenth century for a wealthy landowner. It had since been turned into a hotel with a very nice bar. The beautiful old building still retained many of its original features, and because of Faedra's love of all things old, she enjoyed coming here if only to soak up the atmosphere and imagine what it must have been like to live there when it was originally someone's home.

"Come on dreamy," Amy snapped her from her thoughts. "Let's go in and get you your first official drink."

She responded with a smile, and they trooped in through an open door way. The heavy oak door had been propped open with an ornamental doorstop. It was such a balmy evening; the owners had decided to let the fresh air in. As they entered the bar Faedra stopped dead upon seeing Faen relaxing at a table in the corner of the room. She narrowed her eyes at him. *How did he get here so quickly?*

"What's wrong, Fae?" Zoë asked, and looked over to where Faedra had turned her attention, then looked back at her with a confused expression. "There's nothing there."

"What? Sorry, nothing I'm fine," she spluttered, and continued to the bar, glancing back at Faen who was giving her a wry smile. She narrowed her eyes at him in response.

"Where'd Amy go?" she asked upon noticing her friend's disappearance.

"Probably to the bathroom," Zoë responded nonchalantly.

A couple of minutes passed, and they had their drinks in hand. Faedra had decided on a nice glass of red wine.

"Hey, you guys you have to come and see this," Amy said as she burst through the door. "They have a new statue back here, it's so cool." She came over and grabbed Faedra by the arm.

Faedra slid reluctantly off her bar stool, and allowed herself to be half dragged by her friend through the door towards the bathrooms.

"Where? I can't see one," Faedra said when the corridor they were in was empty, except for a row of floor to ceiling windows that ran the length of it to reveal the beautiful courtyard outside, complete with fountain.

"It's just through there," Amy pointed to the double doors up ahead.

"Amy, I hope you haven't been snooping around again," Faedra said with a frown.

"Of Course I have, I always snoop," she was proud to admit.

Faedra raised her eyes heavenward. Amy could be so brazen sometimes. Amy and Zoë got to the doors before Faedra, and they each took a handle and pulled the doors open.

Faedra peered into the darkened room. In a heartbeat the lights came on and a chorus of "SURPRISE" rang out loud and clear. She nearly jumped out of her skin, and Zoë surreptitiously grabbed her glass of wine, for which she was grateful otherwise she would have been wearing it all down the front of her dress.

Sprawling in front of her were friends and relatives, spreading all the way to the back of the large banquet room. They wore excited expressions on their faces and most were blowing on party horns, throwing streamers at her, and right at the front stood the perpetrators. Her father, flanked by her Uncle Leo and Nicki. She should have known. That was what her father had been so busy doing all day, organizing a surprise party when she had expressly told him that she didn't want a big deal made of her birthday.

It was already more of big deal than he could ever imagine, she thought derisively.

She stood frozen to the spot for what seemed like an eternity, but was probably only a few seconds. She wasn't quite sure how to react. She felt numb. All these people were here for her, but the one person she wished could have been, wasn't… her mother.

She regained her composure. She wasn't about to embarrass her father, or herself in front of all these people by throwing a hissy fit. She took a deep breath and plastered a smile on her face, one she would have to fake for the rest of the evening, of that she had no doubt. Everyone cheered when she smiled, and she saw her father heave a sigh of relief.

The music started and everyone dispersed and started to mingle. When she thought no one was looking, she narrowed her eyes at her father and made a beeline straight for him. He flinched, and braced for the worst. Uncle Leo and Nicki stood their ground next to him.

"Dad, you promised," she stated when she reached him.

"Faedra, it wasn't your dad's idea," Leo interrupted, "it was mine."

She shot him a puzzled look. "Why, Uncle Leo? You knew how I felt." She couldn't bring herself to be mean to her uncle, and surprisingly she felt hurt, not angry.

"I did it for your mother," he stated.

She stepped back like someone had just punched her in the gut, and continued to look at him in bewilderment.

"Lillith made me promise to hold a big party for your eighteenth Birthday. She was most insistent about it. So if you want to blame anyone, Fae, blame your mum."

Obviously, she could never blame her mum for anything. She stared at her dad and uncle, tears pricked behind her eyes. Her mother had wanted her to have a party for her birthday, and she was going to make sure she enjoyed herself.

"Sorry," she mumbled at the floor, feeling a little ashamed of herself.

"No apology needed you big goof," Leo said, and grabbed her in a bear hug. "Just make sure you enjoy yourself."

Faedra had a good look around the room when her uncle released her from his iron grip. There were banners all over, announcing 'Happy Birthday' and '18 at last.' A long buffet table, filled with food, stretched the length of one wall. Helium filled balloons were tied to little weights and floated above each of the tables that surrounded the dance floor, and streamers hung from the rafters of the exposed oak beams that were holding up the roof. A DJ was playing music at one end of the room, and people were already on the dance floor dancing.

"You did all this for me?" she asked her dad, uncle and Nicki. They nodded. "Thank you." She opened her arms for a group hug.

"Go on now," her dad said after they were finished with their hug, "go and enjoy yourself." And without further ado Amy and Zoë each took an arm and dragged her towards the dance floor.

Faedra enjoyed herself dancing to all the latest music in the charts, and some of the older stuff that she liked to listen to also. It seemed like a constant stream of people came up to wish her a happy birthday. She greeted each one graciously, and thanked them for coming. Although she had told her dad that she would only have a couple of drinks, they kept being put in her hands by friends and relatives who wanted to buy her one for her birthday. She had managed, very discreetly, to dispose of some of them in the various potted plants that were dotted around the edge of the banquet room. But when she had been caught in conversation with someone, she had found it hard not to take a few sips, and was starting to get a little tipsy.

The music slowed down, and she made her exit off the dance floor. She watched as Amy and her new boyfriend were slow dancing their way around it, and Zoë and her long-standing beau were doing the same. They looked really happy and she smiled at her friends who were enjoying the moment with their respective partners. She turned to go and find someone to talk to, and bumped straight into Faen's chest. She took a step back in surprise, and looked up at him. She hadn't seen him since that time in the bar, and wondered if he was still around. To be honest she had been so distracted by everything going on that she hadn't even thought to look.

"May I have this dance, Ms. Faedra?" he asked politely.

She squirreled around in her mind for a moment. She'd never danced with a man before, except for her dad, and that was when she was little and stood on his shoes while he twirled them both around, and she didn't think that counted in this instance.

"Um, I don't know how," she admitted, sheepishly.

"I do," Faen replied, holding out a hand for her. "May I?"

She felt her cheeks flush and her heart pound. Not only was she a disaster with her power, she was now going to embarrass herself on the dance floor, too.

Faen took hold of her hand in one of his, placed her other hand on his shoulder, and then placed his other hand around her waist. She was too nervous to giggle, but she felt like they should be on an episode of *Dancing with the Stars.* That image disintegrated almost immediately as Faen led her with grace and fluidity around the floor. The other couples that had been dancing were now turning their attention to her and Faen, and had moved to the edge of the dance floor. She noticed that people who had been mingling all over the banquet room were now forming a circle around them, watching them intently. She also noticed that they were now the only couple dancing.

Faedra couldn't ever remember feeling this alive. She felt like she was floating above the dance floor, it didn't even feel like her feet were touching the ground. She looked up at Faen and focused all of her attention on his eyes that were doing the same to hers. She was locked in a moment of sheer tranquility, and wondered if she would ever come down to earth again.

She did, with a bump. As soon as the music finished there was a loud applause that emanated around them, she tore her gaze from Faen's, and looked around her. The whole party had been captivated by their dance, and she scanned their faces. On most she could see pure delight, but when she got to her father, his features screamed concern, and on her friend's, Amy and Zoë, pure confusion.

Oops, she thought, *none of them know about Faen.*

Heck she had only found out about him just over twelve hours ago, and she'd certainly never thought of a story to tell them when just such a thing like this occurred. But then, in all fairness, she hadn't been prepared for a surprise party either. She had been prepared for sitting in the bar, having a few drinks with her friends, while Faen sat inconspicuously in the corner and kept an eye on her. He had failed miserably on the inconspicuous aspect of the evening, and she made a mental note to show him what it meant in the dictionary when they got home.

She looked at her father like a deer caught in the headlights, as he stalked towards her. Her friends following behind him. She would have to think of something quickly.

"Oh no," she whispered.

"Stay calm, Ms. Faedra," Faen whispered back, and put a calming hand on her shoulder.

The crowd that had accumulated around them was now back to mingling, and dancing. Faen had led Faedra off the dance floor after their dance, and they were now standing to one side of it.

"So who's the dark horse then?" Amy said to Faedra, while raking her eyes up and down Faen.

"Are you going to introduce us?" her father said, with a politeness that was laced with just a hint of venom. He had never seen his daughter with a man, especially one as good looking as this one, and she had never mentioned a boyfriend. His father senses were on full alert.

Faedra scanned their faces again, and swallowed hard. She could feel herself starting to tremble. Faen sensed it too, and gently squeezed her shoulder. Her father was not doing a very good job of masking his concern, and her friends were just positively brimming with excitement for her. It was about time she had a boyfriend, she could read it in both of their expressions.

"Um, Everyone, meet uh, F-red." she caught herself at the last second.

Every pair of eyebrows shot up in unison, including Faen's.

"Frederick, I mean. This is Frederick he is a new boarder at the stables. We just met recently." Her hands were getting clammier by the second. Faedra didn't like to lie, and it wasn't something that came easily to her.

"Pleased to meet you, Frederick," Amy said as she took hold of his hand, and shook it with just a little too much enthusiasm.

"Yes, pleased to meet you," Zoë reiterated with a much more graceful shake of his hand. Faen did the noble head bob that he always did when acknowledging people. It was so old worldly, and so completely Faen.

"Frederick," her father said, taking Faen's hand in a firm handshake. He eyed Faen cautiously, and gave him the 'you lay one finger on my daughter and I'll swing for you' glare.

"You can be assured, Mr. Bennett, my intentions are nothing but honorable," Faen responded to her father's unspoken warning.

Faedra cringed, looked up at him, and gave him a silent 'no one says stuff like that anymore, you'll give yourself away'. He just smiled calmly back at her and it took her breath away, as usual.

CHAPTER EIGHT

Faen had caught the interest of Uncle Leo and Nicki, too, and they now wandered over to meet him. Faedra was feeling more and more uncomfortable with her family surrounding them. They were all very polite, but there was no doubt in her mind, it was a thinly veiled inquisition. She started to relax as Faen charmed the pants off them. Answering their questions without so much as a hint of subterfuge, or annoyance. Faedra thought if she had been questioned like him she would be feeling exasperated by now, but she was impressed by how quickly he could think on his feet. Obviously, all his answers were lies.

She excused herself to go and use the bathroom. She needed a break from the surrealism that was surrounding her at that moment, and wandered down the corridor to where they were located. As soon as the door closed behind her, the sound of the music muffled. Once inside the bathroom she looked at herself in the mirror, she was feeling a little tipsy after having one too many drinks handed to her. Wandering back towards the party she stopped to look out of one of the floor to ceiling windows that lined the corridor.

The courtyard was lit up with floodlights that cast a warming glow over the fountain. There was seating surrounding the fountain, and the whole picture looked inviting. So she decided she needed some fresh air to try and clear the fuzzies that were addling her brain, and went to sit out there for a moment. She would be on the soft drinks for the rest of the night she told herself sternly. She stepped outside into the welcoming warmth of the summer night air, wandered over to one of the benches, and sat down. The sound of the music was reduced to a muffled beat in the background now. She leaned back against the bench and soaked in the atmosphere of the courtyard. The fountain was very pretty in its own austere way.

It was an uncomplicated structure, but grand in its simplicity. The water trickling from the top tier, fell into the tier below it, which then cascaded down to the basin at the bottom. People had thrown coins into it, they glinted in the light from the floodlights that illuminated the water, and she wondered if any of their wishes had come true.

A noise coming from beyond the courtyard, towards the rear vehicular entrance of the hotel, distracted Faedra from her thoughts. It was black as pitch over there, out of reach from the floodlights in the courtyard. She didn't think much of it, it was probably just a guest and there were plenty of people milling around this evening. Although, she noticed now that was she completely alone in the courtyard.

"Hello?" she called into the darkness.

"Faedra," a gravelly voice responded.

She didn't recognize it, but that didn't mean much either. There were a number of the party guest's partners here tonight that she had never met before. She rose from the bench and wandered over to the where the voice had come from.

"Hello, is anyone there?" she asked again, squinting her eyes, trying to force them to see into the darkness.

She felt a warming sensation on her ring finger and looked down at it. The symbols on the ring were glowing brightly. *Wear it also and never take it off. It will warn you if danger is near.* She remembered what her mother had written in her letter. The fine hairs on the back of her neck raised and goose bumps flashed up her arms. A chilling cold enveloped her, a cold like she had felt in the woods. She turned to leave but was not quick enough. She didn't see it coming, doubted if anyone could have, it happened so fast.

No longer were her feet on solid ground. They were now dangling at least a foot above it. Something was holding her around the neck, and she grabbed at it in desperation, trying to pull off whatever was holding her. Her eyes widened with horror when her hands were grasping at nothing but thin air, and realized that nothing physical was holding her. How could she fight against an imperceptible force? She kicked out with her feet in all directions, hoping feebly that she could make contact with something and maybe knock it off balance, but again, she made contact with nothing, no one. A spine chilling cackle erupted at her futile attempt to free herself from whatever was holding her captive.

"We have waited patiently for this moment," the voice spoke again with revelry. Whoever it was, they were certainly enjoying themselves.

She looked around wide eyed, trying to see who else made up the 'we' but she couldn't even see what was holding her, let alone anyone else that may have been lurking in the shadows. Faedra could feel the ring on her finger heat up even more. It didn't hurt, but it was a powerful reminder that she was in very grave danger, a fact that hadn't escaped her attention.

"Who are you?" she croaked through the stranglehold on her neck. Her question was answered in an instant, a pair of eyes glowed in the darkness below her. She felt sick, a deep retching, nauseous feeling resonated from the pit of her stomach. "Oh God, a Redcap," she continued through restrained vocal chords.

There was another gravelly cackle, and it turned Faedra's blood to ice. The force holding her began to move her over towards the light from a streetlamp that was on the sidewalk behind the wall of the back entrance to the hotel. Whoever it was that was holding her, backed her up until the circle of light from the streetlamp illuminated them both.

Faedra looked down, terror-stricken, as the figure holding her gradually came into view. Fear couldn't even begin to describe what she was feeling when her eyes sent what they were seeing to her brain. It was grotesque. One of its long sinewy arms was held upwards towards her. Spindly fingers with claw like nails were shaped as through they were gripping something invisible, then she realized they were, her neck. She was hovering at least three feet up and away from the hand that was held out towards her.

The creature couldn't have been much more than four feet tall, but what it lacked in stature, it made up for in repulsiveness. It wore a long, dirty brown leather tunic that came to mid thigh, and was belted at the waist. What looked like steel boots adorned its feet, and they made a small clanking sound as it walked. She remembered the sound from the woods when they had been running, but hadn't been able to put her finger on it at the time.

It had an ominous looking dagger thrust through its belt that was slightly rusty and stained with blood. Its other hand had hold of a menacing looking weapon with a huge axe blade at the top of a long handle that stood at least a foot taller than the Redcap, and was finished off with a spike at the end. It, too, looked well used and blood stained.

Its face was gnarly, like old elephant hide, with black soulless eyes that were no longer glowing now they were in the light. A long crooked nose that protruded out morosely from the center of its face, and the jagged, uneven fangs it had for teeth, which jutted out from its lower jaw were yellowed and rotting. On its head it wore the article for which it was named, a red cap. It fit its head like a glove, and although she didn't want to admit to it, she thought it looked like skin, but not its own skin, someone else's, and it glistened moistly in the light from the streetlamp.

“What do you want from me?” she croaked, scanning the area. She still couldn’t see any more of them.

“Why, the amulet of course,” it spat back at her in disgust, and turned his attention to the necklace dangling from her neck.

“Why?”

“I don’t ask why, I just get to keep my prize…you,” it cackled with delight.

In a flash it had forced her to her knees. She was now almost at the same eye level with the hideous creature as she kneeled in front of it. She wrinkled her nose when it leaned in close to her, and wafted a breath over her face. It smelled repugnant, and she almost threw up right there and then. As much as she wanted to, she couldn’t close her eyes, and stared frozen in time at it, as it examined her closely.

“I can understand why she wants you dead,” it whispered with spine chilling contempt.

“Who wants me dead?” Faedra squeaked.

“That is of no consequence, Custodian,” it replied, its gravelly voice scraping at her skin like a rough piece of sand paper. He laid his axe-like weapon on the floor and took hold of the amulet with his free hand. Faedra wasn’t sure what happened next, but the creature was flung across the darkness. A howl screeched through the air as it made contact with what she assumed was the dumpster. She made to get up and run for her life, but the creature was back on her in a flash. Holding her neck in its actual hand this time and much, much more violently than before. It held the palm of its other hand for her to see.

“The amulet is warded, only you can touch it. It would seem no one else can while you live. So, it looks like I’m going to have to kill you right here to take it from you, and we were looking forward to having much more fun with you than that, but,” and it shrugged its shoulders, “needs must.” There was a glint in its eyes when it said it.

Faedra moved her eyes downward to look at its hand. She couldn't move her head, it was being held too tightly. The palm of its hand had been seared with the pattern from the amulet, burning a permanent brand into its skin.

Her mind whirled as the oxygen was being cut off to her brain. She couldn't die, not here, not now.

"Faen," she shouted through her constricted vocal chords. Nothing more than a hushed whisper emanated from her mouth. "Faen, help me," she said again, futilely hoping that he could somehow hear her or sense that she was in danger. She looked over towards the courtyard, and her heart sank. It was still empty.

She was quickly sinking into blackness; no she couldn't let this happen.

Do something Faedra, she commanded herself. *You need to do something now, or you will die. Right here, right now.*

The thought of what it would do to her father, to find his only daughter's battered remains, lying lifeless behind the hotel, sparked something deep within her. Her fear turned to anger, which in itself turned into the searing sensation of energy flowing through her body. The streetlamp above her flickered.

She opened her eyes and summoned all of the energy she could from her body, then her mind started reaching outside of her skull, searching for other sources. The light above her flickered again, and she took hold of its energy, too, pulling it inside her body and molding it with her own. The bulb in the street lamp shattered, sending a shower of sparks raining to the ground like one of those fancy fireworks she enjoyed watching on Bonfire Night.

She looked straight into the Redcap's eyes.

"Not tonight you don't," her whisper was barely audible as she channeled all the power she was controlling through her palms and slammed it directly at its chest.

The intensity of it threw the Redcap violently back against the dumpster again, but she couldn't control the immensity of the force she had created and it sent her flying backwards also. Her whole body was picked up by it and she was hurled into the wall behind her with brutal propulsion. She caught a glimpse of Faen exiting through the door into the courtyard. He conjured his sword from nowhere and was spinning it in his hand as he moved towards her. There was a blood-curdling crack as her head slammed against the hard stone of the brick wall. She fell limply to the ground.

"Faedra!" she heard Faen shout, just before everything went black.

Faen moved with lightening speed to the darkness of the area behind the hotel. The street lamp was broken now, so the only light emanating there was the dim glow from the floodlights in the courtyard. He moved with stealth over to the Redcap. It looked unconscious but he wasn't taking any chances, and run it through with his sword. Faen mumbled something and the Redcap shimmered and disappeared. He stood up alert, his sword held ready for battle, and he scanned the area for anything else, but couldn't sense anything untoward. In the next heartbeat he was kneeling over Faedra's lifeless body that was now lying face down on the ground.

"No no no, not again, for the love of the Gods, not again," he cried as he carefully turned her over. She felt limp in his hands, just like Lillith had eleven years ago. He examined her face. She had a gash on her forehead, and blood was trickling from it down the side of her face. He gently moved a lock of hair away from it so he could take a better look. It didn't look too deep and it started to heal right in front of his eyes. He heaved a sigh of relief. She was not dead if her body was healing.

"Faedra, can you hear me?" he asked, his voice soft as silk.

She groaned in response. Her eyes flickered open for just a second as she took in his features, and could see the agonized look in his eyes. It nearly broke her heart.

"I'm taking you home," he said, and she felt the ground disappear beneath her.

She attempted to try and comfort him with a smile, and then sank back into the black abyss once more.

***

He made it to her home within moments of lifting her from the cold hard ground, and lowered her cautiously to her bed. He had to check and see if any bones were broken because if they were they had to be set straight or they would heal crookedly. He took each of her limbs and gently straightened them one by one. He watched as the bruises disappeared almost before they had even had a chance to develop. After she had turned of age, the healing process her body possessed became even more efficient. He took hold of each hand and examined her fingers. Nothing seemed to have been broken and he rested them down on either side of her body. He leaned forward and coaxed the tangled strands of hair away from her face and waited.

The energy he had just witnessed her expend probably had as much to blame for her state of unconsciousness than her head being slammed against the wall. He went down into the kitchen and rummaged through the cupboards until he found what he was looking for. He filled a large glass with water, and filled it almost half way with sugar, stirring it until it dissolved. He returned to Faedra's room with it and placed the glass on her nightstand.

A few more moments passed then Faedra sucked in a deep breath, as if she had been underwater and just come up to the surface for air. Her eyes flew open, wide and scared. She scanned her surroundings, saw Faen, who was sitting beside her, and threw her arms around him.

"You are safe now, Ms. Faedra," he said softly, in an effort to calm her. "Here drink this, you need to regain some of the energy you expended," he said, handing her the glass from the nightstand.

"What is it?" she asked. Although she trusted him implicitly, she still liked to know what she was putting in her body.

"Sugar water," he stated.

She drank it without further comment.

"Did you see what I did?" she exclaimed enthusiastically, after she had finished the entire glass.

"Yes, it was most impressive, Ms. Faedra."

She looked around again, a little disoriented. "Wait, how long have I been gone from the party?" she asked, looking down at her torn and dirty dress.

"About fifteen of your minutes I estimate," he replied.

"Oh good grief, I have to get back there."

She pushed herself past him and headed for the closet. She certainly couldn't return dressed like this, her father would freak out.

"That is not a good idea."

"I don't care, Faen, my dad will be worried sick. I don't even have my cell phone, it's in my purse that is still on a table back at the party." She ran over to the home phone that was sitting in its charger on her nightstand, picked it up and started dialing. Making sure to put in the couple of digits needed so that the number wouldn't show on his caller ID. She hoped he would think she was calling from her cell. She couldn't stand the thought of him worrying about her. "I'll call him from here."

"Hello," Henry answered. She could hear the music in the background. Good the party was still in full swing.

"Hey, Dad it's me."

"Fae? Where on earth are you? I was starting to get worried."

"Don't worry, I needed some fresh air and went for a walk in the village."

"On your own?" he exclaimed.

"No, Faen's with me," she cringed as soon as she said his name, and Faen shot her a strained expression

"You went home to get your dog?" her dad asked incredulously.

God she hated lying to her father, and she was hopeless at it.

"I thought he may need to go for a wee," she said cringing again. "I'll be back in a few minutes."

"Fae, you do the oddest things sometimes. I tell you, that dog knows he has you wrapped around his paw."

She raised her eyes to the heavens. *Oh if only he knew*, she sighed.

His tone changed then. "Is Frederick with you? He disappeared about the same time you did."

"Yes, Dad, he's with me. He didn't want me walking alone, so he asked if he could join me." She listened as her dad grumbled something into the phone, but just at that moment a loud song started up in the background and she couldn't make out what he was saying. It was probably for the best. "I'll see you soon," she yelled over the din.

"You are going to have be more careful what you say in the future, Ms. Faedra," Faen said, stating the obvious.

She turned to him and squared her shoulders. Whether or not he had looked concerned about her when she was lying in his arms almost dead, he certainly didn't now. He was back to his usual stuffy demeanor, and right now was the wrong time. She had almost been killed tonight, certainly had the stuffing knocked out of her, and she had just about had enough of the self righteous fairy that was intruding on her life.

"Well excuse me for not having my brain firing on all four cylinders after it had been slammed into a brick wall just a few minutes ago," she snapped.

She had been expecting a full blown throbbing migraine after that incident, but as yet nothing had materialized, for which she was relieved.

Faen raised an eyebrow at her outburst, but said nothing for a moment.

"Fred, Ms. Faedra?" he looked at her questioningly. "Do you believe I look like a 'Fred'?"

Faedra's shoulders slumped. No, he most certainly did not look like a Fred. "Give me a break, Faen, it was the only other F word I could think of at the time," she said, raising her eyebrows at him. "But I changed it quickly, I don't think Frederick's too bad though."

Faen was quiet again, watching with interest as Faedra continued to look in her closet for a suitable replacement. She picked a similar styled dress, but this one was a deep forest green with a cream embroidered trim around the hem, and she hoped not too many people would notice. Who was she kidding? This dress looked nothing like the one she was wearing that was now ruined. She held it up and looked over at Faen, eyebrows raised. Faen shot her a puzzled look.

"Out," she snapped, and looked towards the door.

"Oh, yes of course, Ms. Faedra," he uttered before his swift exit.

Faedra mumbled something about ungracious fairies under her breath as she changed into her other dress.

"If you insist we go back to the party, I will not leave your side again," he stated without compromise through the door.

"Whatever," she retorted.

"Even if you have to go to the bathroom!" he added for good measure.

She scowled at the door.

"Okay, I'm ready," she said as she opened the door a few moments later to find him waiting patiently, as usual. She had changed into her other dress, tidied her hair, cleaned the blood from her face with a moist wipe, and touched up her makeup, all with such incredible swiftness it surprised even her. There was just a tiny red mark on her forehead now where the gash had been, and she covered that easily with a little concealer.

"So, do I get to go flying again?" she asked, when they were standing outside. She had missed the first experience due to a lack of consciousness.

"If we are to arrive swiftly, yes."

"Which brings me to my next question," she paused for effect.

"And that would be?" Faen responded.

"If I have this ointment on that is supposed to enable me to see through glamour, how come I still can't see your wings?" That particular point was needling at her now.

Faen gave her one of his wry smiles. "That would be because, how would I say, I ramped up the frequency of mine, so to speak."

"Not fair," she mumbled. He just inclined his head in his annoyingly gracious way and held out his arms.

"May I?" he asked.

"Oh, go on then, if you must," she replied nonchalantly, trying very hard to hide the fact that she was super excited that she was about to go flying with a fairy.

Faen scooped her up in his arms, and she wrapped hers securely around his neck, and they glided gracefully across the field to the village. It took her breath away.

"What if someone sees us?"

"They won't, I have hidden us."

Faedra watched as they skimmed above the rooftops of the houses in the village. It was an exhilarating feeling with the warm breeze blowing on her face and through her hair, but all too quickly they were on the ground again, and walking back through the front entrance to the Old Brewery.

Faedra took a deep steadying breath as they got closer to the party. She knew she had some explaining to do. She had just been for a 'walk' in the village with a man no one had ever met before, and she had changed her dress.

"Well, here goes nothing," she whispered to herself as Faen leaned forward and opened one of the doors to the banquet room for her.

Her father was on her in a flash. "Why did you go wandering off without telling anyone?" he demanded. Then looked down at her dress and narrowed his eyes at Faen who was glued to her side, just like he said he would be.

"I spilled red wine on my other one, Dad, so I nipped home to get changed. I didn't want to spend the rest of my birthday in a stained dress."

He didn't look entirely convinced of her story, but didn't say anything more on the matter either. "Well you're back now, please just let me know if you decide to go walkabout again. You know how I worry about you."

"I know, Dad, I'm sorry, it won't happen again." But something told Faedra that maybe that wasn't a promise she was going to be able to keep in the future, and she suddenly yearned for the uncomplicated life she had lived up until this morning. Where she knew exactly who she was, and where she was going.

CHAPTER NINE

Faedra was hoping that no one had noticed the fact that she had devoured almost half of the contents on the buffet table upon her return. She had no idea how many calories her body had literally burned earlier that night, but her body was screaming at her in no uncertain terms, to replenish them. She was starving, and couldn't get the food down quick enough.

"Feeling a bit peckish tonight are we?" Amy said jovially as she crept up behind Faedra, making her jump. "That must be at least your sixth plate of food."

Rats, someone did notice. "It's my Birthday," Faedra replied blankly, she couldn't for the life of her think of anything else to say.

"Well remember, a moment on the lips, lifetime on the hips," Amy said with a smirk. Faedra narrowed her eyes at her friend, and Amy just shrugged in response and gave her a wink.

The party wound down gradually after that, and Faedra said more "goodbyes" and "thank you for comings" than she cared to remember. It was half past midnight before they got home.

Faen was waiting in his dog form at the front door when they arrived. He had left as Frederick the same time she and her father had.

"That was a wonderful party, Dad," Faedra said as she gave him a hug. "Thanks."

"You're welcome, darling. I'm glad you enjoyed yourself. Well, it's been a long day, I'm off to bed. Goodnight." He kissed her on the forehead and made his way to bed.

"Night, Dad."

Faedra and Faen made their way to Faedra's room, too. She was exhausted and looking forward to a good night's sleep. She wasn't going to forget her eighteenth birthday in a hurry, that was for sure.

After she had changed into her pajamas, she let Faen into her room. He was still in his dog form. She climbed into bed and fell asleep almost instantaneously.

Faen took his usual position on the rug beside her, but he didn't fall asleep. He was on full alert, listening to every creak and groan the old house made at night. He knew that the house was warded and nothing could get to Faedra here, but he was extremely concerned about the blatant attack on her at the hotel. He had no idea why the Redcaps were interested in her or who they were in allegiance with, but he was determined to find out.

He was pulled from his thoughts by a noise that Faedra was making above him in her bed. He sat up and watched her for a moment in the glow of a soft light he had created over her head. She was still asleep, but her body was starting to move agitatedly under the covers. Her hairline was wet with sweat, and her eyes, under their lids, were moving about erratically. She was having a nightmare. It didn't surprise him, she had battled a Redcap and lived to tell the tale. Not many Fae could say that, let alone a human.

He blurred into his true form and stood over her. Maybe he could calm her dreams if he could comfort her somehow without waking her up. He frowned when he realized he didn't know how. Tentatively he moved his hand towards her face. His fingers hovered above her forehead for a moment, and then he drew them away again. He hated to see her in distress, but felt powerless to do anything about it.

Her face contorted then, and she started mumbling incoherently. The mumbling got louder and louder until he thought she was going to scream. It was an automatic response, he put his hand over her mouth just as she did, in fact, scream. He had managed to muffle it, knowing that it would have woken her father if he had not.

Faedra was flung from her nightmare by the built in shut off mechanism that everyone has in their brain, to wake them from a nightmare before it gets too intense and you can't escape it. Her eyes were wide with fear again, and they looked down at the hand that was covering her mouth, and then up at Faen in confusion.

"You are safe, Ms. Faedra, you were having a nightmare. You screamed, and it would have woken your father," Faen's voice was a soft whisper.

She nodded her head in understanding, and he lifted his hand from her mouth. She sat up and looked at him with a blank expression. At first she felt numb, but then it started, a slow tremble from the center of her body that quickly intensified to a violent shake. Her teeth started to chatter, and her whole body shook uncontrollably from head to toe. She was suddenly freezing. Her lips turned blue and felt numb, but there was sweat beading on her forehead.

Faen could see what was happening. He had not witnessed it in The Fae, but he had seen it in humans. She was going into delayed shock. He had been amazed at the resilience she had shown after her attack earlier on, but she had been so focused on getting back to the party so her father would not worry, that she hadn't given herself time to digest what had just happened to her. Now, several hours later, her brain and body were telling her it was time to do just that.

"Ms. Faedra," he whispered calmly. "I believe you are experiencing what humans call delayed shock."

She just stared at him, almost like she was looking through him and didn't quite see or hear him. He raised his hand and rested it on her forehead. She felt like ice to the touch. He grabbed her bathrobe from the chair and wrapped it around her shoulders. "Can I get you anything?" he asked with growing concern. "Is there anything else I can do?"

She was still shivering fiercely when she looked him in the eye. "I… don't... want... you. I… want... my... dog." Her words came out in a forceful staccato.

He didn't hesitate, in the blink of an eye he had blurred into his dog form and was sitting beside her on the bed. She looked at her dog for a split second before throwing her arms around his neck and burying her head in his soft welcoming fur. She closed her eyes and held him tight, hoping to get some comfort from him. Hoping that warmth would soon seep back into her soul.

Her brain was telling her that the dog she loved so much was still the detached fairy she couldn't quite work out, but she didn't care. Her heart told her that this was her best friend. That he had always been there for her, wagging his tail when she was happy, letting her do just this when she was sad. Right now, she was downright terrified and confused, and her brain was having a hard time processing it all. So burying her face in Faen's fur was exactly what she needed at that moment.

She regained her composure with surprising alacrity. Only a few moments had passed before the shivering abated, and the shock surging through her felt like it was flowing out through her body and melting into the bed covers. She pulled back from Faen and looked deeply into his molten amber eyes.

"Thank you," she whispered and laid a delicate kiss on his cold wet nose. "You can come back now, I need to talk to you."

He blurred back to his Fae form. The soft amber eyes that were gazing at her only a second before, where now a startling liquid blue, and she drew in a breath. She felt as if someone had just torn her friend away from her. She straightened herself up, ready to get down to business.

"It wanted the amulet," she stated. "Why would it want the amulet?"

He shook his head. "I do not know what a Redcap would want with it, they are killing machines nothing more, nothing less. As long as they have fresh blood on their caps they are happy."

Faedra cringed. She remembered the way its cap had glistened moistly in the light from the streetlamp, and realized that had been someone's fresh blood. Her body gave an involuntary shudder.

"They must be working for someone. Although they are mostly solitary creatures, they have been known to band together and do someone else's bidding, if the prize was right," he continued.

"Who else would want the amulet? The letter said it was no more powerful than a pretty trinket without the Book of Anohs, and that's supposedly under immense protection. Can anyone get their hands on the book?" she asked.

"The book is bound under heavy protective magic, only the Keeper of the Book and the king have access to it," he replied. "Did the Redcap say anything else?"

"Yes," she whispered, and lowered her eyes.

"What?"

"It said, I can understand why she wants you dead," she spoke flatly, bringing her eyes back up to meet Faen's. She watched a look of concern flash across his face, but then it was gone again. "Who would want me dead, Faen? No one is supposed to even know about me, and what could I have possibly ever done to any of your kind that they would want to kill me?"

What he did next surprised her. He leaned forward and cupped her face in his hands. His eyes, now just a few inches from hers, shone brightly with their intensity and determination.

"I do not know, Ms. Faedra but I will find out, and I will keep you safe. Of that you have my word." He let his hands linger for just a fraction more than was needed, then his eyes flickered as though he were snapping himself out of a trance, and he pulled them away.

"There's something else, too," she continued. "In the graveyard I saw three pairs of eyes, tonight I only saw one creature. That means there are still two more of those things out there after me." She swallowed hard.

"Tomorrow you will stay within the property boundary, you will be safe here. I will go and try to find out all that I can. Now, you must sleep, Ms. Faedra, your body needs to rest." He looked at the light he created over Faedra's pillow and it disappeared, throwing the room into darkness. Fear gripped her by the throat.

"No don't," she cried as she grabbed for his arm.

The light came on again instantly, shining a soft glow over her features. Her eyes were frightened and pleading. He looked at her with understanding and nodded his head.

"As you wish, Ms. Faedra," he said with a warm smile. He could hardly blame her for being scared of the dark now.

She lay her head back down on the pillow. She didn't know if he spent the rest of the night watching over her as man or dog. She was asleep as soon as her head hit the pillow.

***

The morning came far too quickly for Faedra's liking. She rolled over to look at her clock. "What time is it?" she mumbled to herself as she stretched.

"Ten o'clock in the morning, Ms. Faedra."

She nearly jumped out of her skin, and looked to the end of her bed. Faen was sitting there, dressed in his fae attire once more. Her shoulders slumped.

"It wasn't just a bad dream after all, was it?" she asked dejectedly.

"No, Ms. Faedra, it was not."

She could hear the muffled sounds of the television coming from the living room below her. Her dad had probably been up and around bright and early, and had let her sleep in. He likely thought she would be suffering from a hang over this morning, but she was pleased to be feeling surprisingly clear headed. She heard the latch lift on the living room door.

"Fae, are you awake?" Henry called up the stairs.

"Just about," she called back.

"You have to come and see this, something really weird is happening."

She looked at Faen with a 'what now?' expression plastered all over her face. Extricating herself from the bedcovers, she threw her bathrobe on over her pajamas. Faen blurred into his dog form and jumped off the bed to follow her out the door. She stopped dead at the top of the stairs. He hadn't been anticipating that, and bumped right into the back of her legs. She turned slowly to look out of the window. Faen nudged her leg - he couldn't risk changing into his true form outside of her room - to ask her what was wrong. She looked down at him then back out of the window.

"Look," she pointed out the window.

He stood on his hind legs, rested his front paws on the windowsill, and looked in the same direction as her.

"The leaves are turning. It's still summer, they shouldn't be turning for another couple of months yet." They looked at one another, turned, and nearly fell over each other going down the stairs in their haste to get to the living room.

Her dad was sitting in his chair, cupping a mug of tea in his hands. He was glued to the television, completely mesmerized.

"It's the same thing on every channel," he stated, tearing his eyes away from the screen for just a second then returning them directly. "They thought at first it was a group of activists spraying weed killer. Like that time, a few years back, when the activists burned fields of genetically modified crops in protest. But now it's happening all over the world, and no one can explain it."

Faedra perched herself on the edge of the sofa. Faen sat by her feet, and they were both very still. They watched while the news anchor described the phenomenon unraveling all over the world. It had started last night in England, but quickly spread throughout Europe, then to Asia, Australia, and now America. Crops were dying. Huge swaths of agricultural fields were being wiped out.

"If this continues, the world will be facing a famine of global proportions," the newsreader's grave voice told the viewers.

Faedra's jaw dropped. She caught sight of something out of the corner of her eye, and turned to look outside. The leaves were starting to fall. Something was very very wrong.

She looked down at Faen, and he looked up at her. They subtly nodded heads as if they were having a conversation only they could hear, and she jumped up and headed back to her room, followed closely by him.

"Where are you going in such a hurry?" Henry asked. "This is serious stuff going on here," he continued, pointing at the television.

"I know, Dad, but it's a beautiful day outside and I'd like to take advantage of it. I'm going to take Gypsy out for a ride. Besides, there's nothing I can do about it," she inwardly cringed at how callous she sounded.

"Oh the frivolity of youth," he muttered, but she was already charging up the stairs to her bedroom.

"What on earth's going on?" she spoke in a harsh whisper to Faen as he blurred between forms, and wondered if he could hear when he was half in, half out, so to speak.

"This is very grave, Ms. Faedra." Apparently he could hear between forms. "I have to get to Azran and see Elvelynn."

She looked at him incredulously. "No, *we* have to get to Azran," she stated without compromise, "and who's Elvelynn?"

"Elvelynn is the Keeper of the Book of Anohs, and it is too dangerous for you outside of your home."

"The Redcaps chasing me, are here, not in Azran, and you promised me you wouldn't leave my side remember? How can you keep me safe if you're not around?"

He could see by the determined glare she was shooting at him he didn't think he was going to win this battle, and besides she did have a point. He was not happy at the thought of leaving her alone either.

"Okay, you may come with me," he conceded, "but we have to hurry."

She ran to her closet and tore out some clothes. She looked at him, they were in a hurry she didn't have time for formalities.

"Eh, just turn around a minute," she instructed.

He did so without hesitation. She threw her clothes on at breakneck speed, and was ready in about thirty seconds flat.

Faen blurred again into his dog form, and they ran back down the stairs and into the living room. Trying to steady their pace in front of her father so he wouldn't be too suspicious.

"We're off now, Dad. See you later," she said as chirpily as she could muster, and leaned over to kiss him on the cheek.

"But you haven't had any breakfast."

"I'll grab some on the way," she called over her shoulder as her and Faen exited to the porch.

"It's Sunday, there isn't..." they were gone, "anything on the way," Henry continued to himself and shrugged his shoulders. His daughter was certainly starting to act strangely the past couple of days.

Faedra and Faen jumped into her car, and she heaved a sigh of relief when the engine roared into life on the first try.

Well it was more of a meow than a roar, but she wasn't complaining.

Faen blurred into his true self and climbed over to sit in the front seat beside her.

They drove in silence for a few moments, passing a couple of cornfields as they did. Faedra glanced over at the corn that should have been lush and green but was brown and dying.

"Someone's stolen the Book of Anohs, haven't they?" she asked with trepidation. Faen didn't respond. "Haven't they?" Faedra insisted.

"We do not know that for sure, Ms. Faedra."

"Well it would explain why someone wants the amulet, and seems quite happy to kill me to get it."

"Yes, that would be a logical conclusion," he agreed, then sighed. "Can this car go any faster?"

"You tell me, Faen. You've ridden in it since I got it, you should know." Where had she gotten all this sarcasm from all of a sudden. A few days ago she would never have dreamed of being rude to anyone, but she was firing off at Faen left, right and center. Maybe it was the fact that she was worried about a pending global famine, or it could just be the effect he had on her. She couldn't quite decide which and kept the thought to herself.

"Oh no, it's Sunday," she cried as they pulled into the church car park. It was full.

"Yes, Ms. Faedra we have already surmised that fact," he shot her a bewildered glance.

"Which means that there will be loads of people around. People that might see something they shouldn't," she was exasperated. Did she have to spell it out for him?

"They will only see what I wish them to see."

"And what about me?"

"As long as we are touching, the glamour will hide you too," he explained as if she should already have known that fact.

"Oh."

Faedra sandwiched her little old car in between a couple of bright shiny new ones. Faen got out of the car and was round to her side, opening the door for her before she had even pulled the keys out of the ignition. His manners were impeccable, she certainly couldn't fault him for that.

"Thank you." She at least hadn't forgotten her manners either.

"You are most welcome," he nodded his head graciously.

"Um, Faen, you are wearing your old worldly clothing again. You'll stick out like a sore thumb, not to mention that carrying a lethal weapon in England is against the law." She eyed his sword intently as she tried to sound as diplomatic as possible under the circumstances.

"No one can see me, Ms. Faedra."

"Great, so now I look like I'm talking to myself?" She closed the car door, and shoved the keys in the front pocket of her jeans.

He gave her one of his wry smiles and took her hand. "No, now only I can see you, talking to me."

She looked down at their intertwined fingers and found herself at a loss to understand why someone who irked her the way he did, had the ability to send bolts of electricity up her arm and straight to her heart. He looked down and caught her staring at their hands.

"Is there a problem, Ms. Faedra?"

She felt her cheeks flush. "No, no problem."

"Then come, the portal is this way. We must find Elvelynn," he started with determination in the direction of the graveyard gate.

Faedra held her breath as a couple of people walked straight past them, but didn't even glance their way. "People can't hear us either?" she asked.

"No they cannot."

As soon as they entered through the gate, the friendly black and white collie bounded over to see them. Faedra beamed at it when it gave her its usual toothy grin. It felt good to see a friendly face.

"She is of age now, Jocelyn, you may show yourself." When Faen spoke his voice was laced with just a hint of irritability.

Faedra stood upright sharply, as in the blink of an eye the collie shimmered in front of her and was replaced by the most beautiful girl she had ever set eyes on. She noticed that when Jocelyn changed form it was a distinct shimmer, compared to Faen who blurred into his form, and she fleetingly wondered if it had anything to do with being a male or female fae.

She took a step back and gasped. She couldn't help herself, and wondered if all fae were as beautiful as these two. Jocelyn stood a few inches shorter than Faedra, and looked younger too, although she knew in actual years she was probably much older. But she estimated that Jocelyn looked about fifteen or sixteen years old. She had flawless, luminescent skin that almost sparkled in the sunlight. Striking, liquid blue eyes, like her brother's, with long dark lashes that framed them to perfection, smiled at her warmly.

She also took on similar coloring to her dog form. Her hair, that was long and sleek, flowed halfway down her back. It was almost all black with the exception of a band of white blonde at the front of her head, which had been braided into delicate braids. The braids had been intricately woven through the remainder of her hair creating a unique lace effect pattern. She wore a gorgeous black and white dress, with a fitted bodice and flowing skirt that came to mid calf with a handkerchief style hem. But the thing that took Faedra's breath away, was that Jocelyn did not care to hide her wings like her brother did, and Faedra realized that she had been quite blatantly gaping at them with her jaw dropped for a moment now. She snapped it shut, and hoped she hadn't looked too rude.

Jocelyn's wings, that rhythmically opened and closed at a slow steady pace, reminded Faedra of someone subconsciously tapping a foot or drumming their fingers on a table. They weren't beating fast enough to lift her from the ground, but rather she looked like a resting butterfly that opened and closed its wings while perched on a petal. They reached at least two feet taller than her shoulders and each one spanned another good body width wide, to either side of her. They were made up of four sections. The upper, larger sections were white, and the lower, smaller sections were black, and shaped into a teardrop at the lower outside corner just like one of those exotic butterflies that she had only ever seen in a book, or on the Animal Channel. Her wings as a whole had a luminescent quality to them also, and shimmered enchantingly in the sunlight.

"Wow," Faedra breathed.

"Hello, my name is Jocelyn." Her voice was high pitched and musical, and she spoke with excitement dripping from every word. "It is so good to be able to actually talk to you at last, I cannot believe you have finally turned of age. I was starting to get so impatient, I nearly gave myself away on several occasions," she giggled and a flush came to her cheeks.

"Err…" Faedra started to talk, even though she was pretty speechless at that moment. Faen interrupted, but that didn't stop her from scowling at him for being rude to his sister.

"Jocelyn," Faen said bluntly, "there will be plenty of time for small talk later, we need to see Elvelynn."

"Ooh, Elvelynn," Jocelyn squealed. "I have not seen Elvelynn for an eternity. Can I come with you?"

"You saw her not more than a moon's phase ago, and no you cannot come with us. We are going on business."

"Oh, Brother, please. You have to let me come, can I come, please?" The musical sound of her voice as it went up and down the octaves as she spoke, reminded Faedra of a cat walking on a piano keyboard.

"The answer is still no." Faen was frowning at her now, and moved to walk Faedra past her.

"But I'm Bored!" she exclaimed with a pout as she stomped her foot.

Faedra's eyebrows rose at her outcry. "Wow, fae get tantrums too?" she whispered to Faen.

"Only the spoiled ones," he replied.

"Please?" Jocelyn made one last attempt, with shiny tear pricked eyes.

That did it, Faedra was on her side. She always was a sucker for anyone who cried, and she had taken an instant liking to Faen's little sister. She also knew she would probably get a lot more conversation from the young fairy than she would from her brother, and had visions of this being another very long day.

"Oh, go on, Faen. Let her come with us, it will be one more person to watch over me. Especially if I'm as prized as you seem to believe I am."

He hesitated, sighed, and frowned. "Alright, Jocelyn, you may journey with us to Elvelynn's. But you must come straight back here and continue your duty."

"Yes," Jocelyn cried in victory as she clapped her hands together a couple of times then held them up to her lips like she was getting ready to pray. Her eyes sparkled with excitement. "Thank you, Brother. I will not get in your way, I promise." She planted a kiss on his cheek and he rolled his eyes.

CHAPTER TEN

"Are you alright, Faedra? You look a little pale," Jocelyn asked as they moved forward down the path.

"I think I'm about to have a meltdown," Faedra replied.

"Don't be silly, Faedra, you are human. Humans do not melt, not that I have ever witnessed."

"It's a figure of speech, Jocelyn. Two days ago I was a normal – well I admit some odd things had been happening to me, but that's beside the point – seventeen year old. Then yesterday, bam, I turn eighteen and all of a sudden I find out that I descend from an ancient Celtic bloodline, who were once fae themselves. My dog morphs into a man in my bedroom, scaring the living daylights out of me, and turns out to have been a fae all along. I am Custodian of an ancient fae amulet that has the power to control weather. I get attacked by an evil, murderous Redcap, and more are still after my blood, and I'm about to step through an invisible door into another world, your world. So please excuse me if I quietly have a meltdown." She admitted to herself that she was being a tad melodramatic at that point.

"My dear Faedra, there was nothing much quiet about that," Jocelyn snickered.

"You get the gist though?" Faedra grinned.

Jocelyn gave her a warm smile, put an arm around Faedra's shoulders, and gave her a squeeze. "I think we are going to be great friends," she stated.

Faen rolled his eyes again and held up is arm to direct Faedra towards the portal. "Come, the portal is up ahead."

She couldn't see anything, even when she squinted her eyes. All she saw was the gravel path laid out ahead of them. They had only walked a few yards when Faen and Jocelyn came to a stop. Faedra had no choice in the matter, her hand was still being held by Faen's. She had to confess it reminded her of the way she used to feel when her father held her hand as a child. It was strong and sure, and made her feel safe, and dare she admit, cared for.

Jocelyn stood on the path in front of them and said something in a language that Faedra was sure she had never heard before. She looked with bewilderment up at Faen.

"She was speaking an incantation to open the portal," he replied to her unspoken question.

"But if you need an incantation to open it, and it's definitely not in English, why would you need to guard it?" she asked Jocelyn.

"Because, my dearest Faedra, some silly person got drunk one night," Jocelyn replied. Although she spoke in her usual musical voice, Faedra could sense she was somewhat disgruntled by that fact. Faedra looked at her blankly.

"Many years ago a man was walking through the church yard as a short cut on his way home from the pub, he was very drunk and talking to himself. When he got to where the portal was his slurred speech sounded similar to the incantation. The portal opened and he walked straight into Azran."

Faedra's eyebrows shot up. "I bet that caused a stir."

"Somewhat," Jocelyn continued. "He had been walking around Azran for a while, watching us flying around and going about our business before one of the king's sentries spotted him. They carefully extricated him through the portal back to your world, but the vision stuck with him. Luckily because he was so drunk no one believed him, but it started, what do you call it, an urban legend?"

Faedra nodded. "I've heard about that legend. Wow, so that really happened?"

Jocelyn nodded. "Every now and then someone will try and see if there is anything to the legend, and try and get through the portal. No one has succeeded since, but the king decided that he was not willing to take the chance on another human accidentally stumbling into our world. I was assigned to guard it and make sure only those who should, could pass."

Faedra thought it best not to admit to the fact that she had considered trying it out when she was younger, but had never gotten around to it.

"It's open," Jocelyn said, and motioned for them to follow her. A second later she disappeared right in front of Faedra's eyes. Faen stepped forward to continue after her but Faedra was glued to the spot, staring fixatedly at where Jocelyn had just vanished. Her heart started to pound, and she found herself feeling incredibly nervous. What would they find on the other side? Did it hurt traveling between realms? Would she be able to get back home? She felt Faen give her hand a gentle, reassuring squeeze. She searched his eyes and found reassurance there, too.

"You will be fine, Ms. Faedra. I will not let go of you."

She gave him a feeble smile and allowed him to lead her forward. At that moment she had an epiphany. She knew without doubt that she would follow him to the ends of the earth, his or hers, it didn't matter anymore. She took a deep breath and closed her eyes.

"We are through, Ms. Faedra," Faen whispered in her ear.

Well that was quick, she thought. *Somewhat of an anticlimax really.* She was thankful that there was no pain, just a tingle that shot through her whole body, but was gone almost instantly. She exhaled and opened her eyes. Her jaw dropped again. She had a feeling that was going to be happening quite frequently in the foreseeable future.

They had just walked through an ornate stone archway. It was similar to the one at the entrance to the cathedral grounds near her home in Norwich, and they were now standing in a tropical paradise. Although Faedra had never actually been to a tropical paradise, this is how she imagined it would look. Minus the ornate stone archway that looked somewhat out of place standing alone in the vegetation. They were surrounded by lush forest, and flowers of all shapes and colors carpeted the ground. The air smelled so sweet she thought she would be able to stick out her tongue and taste it. Up ahead, a waterfall cascaded into a deep aqua pool of crystal water, which flowed into a stream that meandered past where they were standing. She looked into it and could see brightly colored fish swimming around. A couple of the fish jumped up out of the water and made small splashes as they dove back in.

"You live *here*?" she asked Faen and Jocelyn, her voice full of wonder.

"Welcome to the Land of Azran, Ms. Faedra," Faen announced with grandeur.

Jocelyn looked very pleased with Faedra's response to her world. A world she was obviously very proud of.

A rustle in the bushes distracted them and all three turned their heads at the same time. Faen drew his sword halfway out of its sheath and then slid it back in when the creature making the rustling noise appeared. He was a tiny man with a squat face and big pointy ears. He had rosy cheeks and kind eyes, a leprechaun perhaps.

"Todmus, my friend." Faen walked over to greet the little man.

"Mr. Faen, it's always a pleasure to welcome you back to Azran," Todmus said with a sincere smile.

"Todmus we need to travel to the City. Do you have three horses we can borrow?" Faen asked the little man.

"Yes, Mr. Faen," he snapped his fingers. "They will be ready momentarily." Then he cast his gaze over to Faedra, and his eyes grew wide when they rested on the amulet. "So the legend is true?"

"It is, Todmus, but I know I can rely on your discretion in this matter."

"You can trust me, Sir, I did not see or hear anything."

"Thank you, Todmus. You have long been a faithful friend and loyal citizen." Faen said as he patted the small man on the back.

"This way, Sir," Todmus motioned for them to go through the small opening in the bushes. Faen went first and Jocelyn last, sandwiching Faedra in the middle. Faedra had a feeling she was going to be a fairy sandwich on several occasions throughout their journey to Elvelynn's.

They walked a short distance on a narrow winding path through some dense vegetation, until they came to an opening. There waiting for them were three pure white horses.
Faedra sucked in a breath. "Oh, beautiful." she breathed as they wandered over to the horses.

She stood beside one and stroked its neck. It's hair felt as soft as silk to her fingers.

Faen wandered up beside her. "Here, put this around your neck," he said as he conjured a beautiful silk scarf out of nowhere and tied it gently around Faedra's neck. "Not everyone in Azran is as trustworthy as Todmus."

Faedra looked down at the scarf, it covered the amulet nicely. "Thank you."

Faen inclined his head and gave her a leg up to mount her horse. She watched as he walked round to his horse, rose gracefully in the air, and lowered himself onto his saddle. Jocelyn, with a couple of beats of her wings, did the same.

"Err, if you can fly, why are we riding?" Faedra asked.

" We have much ground to cover to get to Elvelynn's. We will ride part of the way and fly the rest," he answered, and without further ado kicked his horse into a gallop and flew off at speed down the dirt trail that exited out the opposite side of the clearing from which they had entered.

"Come on," Jocelyn squealed with excitement, and the two of them galloped off behind her brother.

Jocelyn and Faedra fell into a steady pace behind Faen, who kept the lead. They continued at a gallop for what seemed like a several miles until Faen adjusted their pace to a steady canter. The lush forest flew past them in a blur of green.

"I don't know how much longer my legs will be able to take this," Faedra admitted to Jocelyn after a while. "Most people think that the horse does all the work but my muscles are starting to feel like jelly."

"Brother," Jocelyn called out to Faen, "we need to steady to a walk for a while."

Faen didn't question her. He brought his horse down into a trot then slowed to a walk, Faedra and Jocelyn followed suit.

"Thank you," Faedra said with relief, to her friend.

"Do not mention it," Jocelyn replied with a warm smile.

Faen kept the lead several yards up ahead of them, and Faedra noticed his head scanning the woods from side to side. It was obvious that he was keeping a lookout for anything untoward, which left her and Jocelyn able to talk. They fell into easy conversation. Jocelyn was very amiable, Faedra felt like they had been friends for a long time, and in an odd way they had.

"Jocelyn?" Faedra asked after a lull in their conversation.

"Yes?"

"What's with the wings?" she continued, nodding in Faen's direction.

Jocelyn drew her eyebrows together in confusion. "I do not understand."

"Your brother, he hides his wings. Haven't you noticed?"

"Glamour does not work on us, Faedra. I see his wings just as I always have, but he hides them from you?"

"Yes. He won't let me see them, but won't give me a reason why."

She gave her brother's back a knowing smile. "That is very interesting."

"It is, why?"

"What do you think of Azran so far?" Jocelyn said lightly, trying to steer the conversation down a different path.

"Don't try and change the subject, Jocelyn. Why is it interesting?" Faedra pressed.

Jocelyn sighed. "I should not have said anything."

"Oh don't you start, I've been hearing that a lot lately," she thought back to Rose at the festival. "I'll keep pestering until you tell me."

Jocelyn looked thoughtful for a while. She was trying to find the best way to explain what she wanted to say. "It is very rare for a fae to have feelings for a human, but if that should ever happen we tend to be very cautious about it," she paused, and looked to see how Faedra was digesting the information so far. Faedra was engrossed, hanging on Jocelyn's every word.

"Go on," Faedra encouraged.

"Well if we were to have feelings for a human, we would want to know that those feelings were mutual before we would show our wings."

Faedra looked at her in obvious confusion.

"Let me see, how do I explain this?" Jocelyn continued.

She looked around as if she would get the inspiration from the trees or the sky. "Ah yes, I know. In The World of Men it would be like someone who is rich, having feelings for someone who is poor. The rich person would want to make sure that their feelings were reciprocated because of who they really were, and not just because they had lots of money. Therefore they might have a tendency to hide that fact until they knew for sure that the poor person liked them despite of, and not because of, the fact they were rich."

"Ah, I think I understand what you are getting at," Faedra nodded in response to Jocelyn's explanation.

"You see, our wings have a tendency to, how shall I say, enchant humans."

Faedra gazed at Jocelyn's stunning wings again for the umpteenth time. She had to admit she was having a hard time taking her eyes off them. They were indeed enchanting.

"I see what you mean," she agreed.

She let the information sink in for a moment. Faedra was one of those people that would get the punch line of a joke a minute after everyone else had finished laughing at it. "Hold on a minute," she searched Jocelyn's face while she spoke. "Are you saying that Faen has feelings for me?"

Jocelyn just smiled warmly.

"But you must be wrong on this one. I know for a fact that he doesn't," Faedra stated bluntly, looking at Faen's back.

"Are you so sure, Faedra?" Jocelyn asked.

"Yes, I'm sure. He always acts as though it's an inconvenience to be lumbered with looking after me," Faedra insisted.

"My dear Faedra, my brother has been with you every step of your life for the past eleven of your years. He has had the very rare opportunity to spend time with you when you thought no one was watching. You have been at your most uninhibited in those times. You, shall we say, have completely enchanted him."

"So answer me this then. Why does he act so detached around me all the time?"

"I cannot answer that, Faedra, but I am sure he has his reasons."

Faedra turned her eyes forward to gaze at Faen who was still several yards ahead of them. She thought for a while about what Jocelyn had just divulged to her then shook her head. *No, she must be mistaken.*

They rode in silence for a while. Faedra was in a daydream, still trying to absorb what Jocelyn had told her. She wasn't quite sure how long they had been riding in silence, but was torn from her thoughts by a gasp that resonated from beside her. She turned to look at Jocelyn and was shocked to see the look of horror on her friend's face.

"What it is, Jocelyn? What's wrong?" Faedra asked, but she didn't need Jocelyn to answer. She could see for herself what had shocked her friend. "Oh no, not here too."

Her heart sank as she observed that the forest around them was dying. Some of the trees still had green leaves, some had leaves that were turning, and some were already devoid of all foliage. They had just walked from summer to winter in just a few paces. Up ahead of them all the trees were bare, the grass was brown, and the flowers were wilted and shriveled. The air didn't smell sweet anymore either, there was a dank mustiness to it now, and Faedra could taste its sourness on the back of her throat as she breathed in.

Up ahead she could see an opening in the trees. When they eventually reached it they came to a stop side-by-side, and she gaped open-mouthed once more. They were standing on the edge of a valley. Laid out below them, and as far as the eye could see was brown, dying countryside. There was a city in the distance. It looked like a good-sized city, with a castle that stood proudly in the middle. She could sense that this view would have usually held such radiance it probably would have taken her breath away. As it was, she wanted to weep at its lifelessness. Jocelyn did weep, big fat tears rolled down her cheeks and splashed onto her dress.

"Oh, Brother, what has happened here?" Jocelyn asked Faen.

"I do not know, Jocelyn, but I fear the worst," he replied stoically.

"The castle, it does not sparkle anymore," she cried.

Faedra looked at the castle in the distance. It did indeed have a lackluster appearance. She could see the remnants of its grandeur, and imagined it sparkling when it was in its previous condition, but right now everything, including the castle, looked insipid.

"We fly from here. The horses will find their way back to Todmus," Faen announced as he stepped down from his horse with a grace that was not lost on Faedra.

Faedra took both of her feet out of the stirrups, and jumped down from her horse as she always did back home. Not the most graceful of dismounts, but the one she had been taught from her very first riding lesson, and old habits die hard. Jocelyn lowered herself down with a couple more beats of her wings. They stood still, hardly daring to breathe as they looked over the dying valley spread out ahead of them. Before Faedra even had time to register what 'we fly from here' meant to her, she had an arm wrapped around each of hers, and was being launched off the side of the valley wall, which up until this point she hadn't considered to be that steep.

"You could at least warn me when you are going to do stuff like this," she squeaked as her heart lurched into her mouth and her stomach did cartwheels.

The wind blew in her face and whipped through her hair. Jocelyn had hold of one arm and Faen the other, and they were looking ahead, concentrating hard. She had to admit it was the most incredible feeling to be flying outside of a plane. A bit like being on an amusement park ride without being strapped in. She couldn't decide at that point if the queasy feeling in her stomach was a product of just being launched off the side of a hill, or the fact that her heart was saddened by the devastation below them.

They were flying low to the ground now and she could see close up how dead everything looked. The queasy feeling developed into a definite knot in her stomach, and her question was answered. Thoughts of the book flew through her mind almost as quickly as the ground flew beneath her. The realization that something had happened to the book was quickly taking shape and that didn't bode well for anyone in any realm, least of all hers. Remembering what her mother had said in the letter, that combining the book and the amulet would give the user the ultimate power to control not just plant life, but the weather, too. Whoever had the book had made it very clear that they were going to get their hands on the amulet, too, only that could not be accomplished unless she were dead.

She closed her eyes and tried to change the subject that had now taken on an obsessive quality in her brain. She felt herself being moved and opened her eyes to see that Faen had taken hold of her, and was carrying her as he did last night when they had returned to the party. She quickly wrapped her arms around his neck and gave him a questioning look.

"Jocelyn was growing tired," he answered. "She is not used to carrying extra weight when she flies."

"Sorry, Jocelyn," Faedra called over her shoulder.

"There is no need to be, Faedra, I am not as strong as my brother. I am glad I was able to help him up to that point," she said with kindness.

Faedra now understood why they had made part of the journey on horseback. They had an extra body to carry. She assumed it would be much like her trying to carry someone a great distance, and knew for a fact that she wouldn't have had the strength to do it for very long either.

"We don't have too much further, Ms. Faedra," Faen said looking ahead.

Faedra looked in the same direction and could see the city looming closer in front of them. A huge wall encircled the city in a protective manner. It looked medieval, but in a much more beautiful and less rugged way. As they got closer, Faedra could see another ornate stone archway just like the portal, but this one was several times bigger. Jocelyn slowed and lowered herself to the ground just in front of Faen who did the same. He lowered Faedra to the ground, but her legs instantly collapsed underneath her. They had turned to jelly, what with the galloping and the flying, she wasn't sure how much more her body could take that day. In a flash, Faen scooped her up before she had a chance to hit the ground.

"Sorry, Ms. Faedra. I had forgotten the affect flying with us has on humans," he said apologetically. "Your legs should return to normal in just a few minutes."

They stood in front of the archway for a moment, almost hesitant to proceed any further and have their suspicions confirmed. As though if they didn't have them confirmed, everything would go back to how it was. After a moment they walked forward. Faen was still carrying Faedra, and Jocelyn stood closely by their side. The three of them a united front against whatever lay waiting for them on the other side.

Faedra looked up in awe at the underneath of the archway as she was being carried through it. A beautiful mosaic of a fairy kneeling down to admire an exotic flower just like the ones near the portal, adorned the ceiling. They got to the other side of the arch and stopped. Faedra turned her attention to the scene unfolding before her. What she imagined after seeing the mosaic, as once being a peaceful and calming place to live, was in utter turmoil.

"I think my legs will hold me now," she whispered to Faen.

She couldn't be sure but she thought she felt him tremble. This was his home and it was in disarray, it must be having some effect on him. He lowered her to the ground keeping a steadying arm under hers until he was sure she was stable enough to stand on her own.

All three stood side-by-side, just as they had on the edge of the valley, and watched the chaos unfold before their eyes. People were running in all directions, panic and desperation on their faces. Some were crying, some were carrying small children, some had stopped and were looking around them with dazed expressions. What were once quite obviously areas of lush greenery, like miniature parks and gardens, were now brown and dying. The city seemed to be dying from the inside out. A lump developed in Faedra's throat. She was determined that if there was any way she could help restore this majestic place to its former glory, she would move heaven and earth to do so.

CHAPTER ELEVEN

Faen and Jocelyn started walking with an urgency Faedra could physically feel in the air.

"Elvelynn's is this way," he said to her as they made their way through the panicking inhabitants of the city.

Faedra stuck out like a sore thumb in her World of Men clothing, but no one noticed her. They were all too busy trying to make sense of what was happening to their home. There were many different kinds of people running around them. She realized now that not everyone who lived in Azran were what she considered to be fairies. She also recognized what she thought were elves, dwarves, a few pixies and a leprechaun or two amongst them. It wasn't hard to figure out that these peaceful souls had never experienced fear or confusion before, and it broke her heart to see the pain on their faces.

As they made their way through the streets the pandemonium started to settle as the residents made their way into their homes. She looked around to see shutters closing hastily over windows, and doors being slammed shut. It wasn't too much longer before she could see that the three of them were the only ones left walking down the cobbled lanes. An eerie hush lay over the city like a blanket, and it caused the fine hairs on the back of Faedra's neck to stand to attention.

"It is just around the next corner," Jocelyn said, breaking the unearthly silence.

They turned the corner, and out of all the houses that lined the street, Faedra knew instantly which one belonged to Elvelynn. It was the only one with a door and windows that were still wide open and welcoming. It was quite obvious that the inhabitant was not at home.

"Stay here," Faen commanded as they approached.

Jocelyn and Faedra did as he asked, and watched as he drew his sword and stepped with caution through the open door. His sword, which he held out in front of him with both hands, entered first. A moment later he was standing in the doorway, his sword back in its sheath.

"There is no one here," he said with disappointment. "It is safe to enter."

Jocelyn and Faedra didn't hesitate, they walked up to the front door and entered the pretty house. There had once been a climbing rose framing the front door to welcome guests, but this was now all shriveled and dry. Once inside they could see that a struggle had taken place. Faen was standing beside an armoire that was intricately carved with Celtic knot work. The doors were open, and one of them was hanging at an angle on a single hinge. There was nothing inside.

"I take it that's where the Book of Anohs should be," Faedra whispered, although she wasn't quite sure why she was whispering. The atmosphere had such a hushed quality about it she didn't dare speak any louder.

Faen hung his head, it was all the answer she needed, and a shiver ran down her spine. She looked around the room, it, too was in disarray. The chairs were overturned, there was broken glass on the floor, a wilted flower laying in amongst the jagged shards from where a vase had been knocked off the table, and smashed to the ground in an obvious struggle.

"Elvelynn," Jocelyn spoke with a catch in her voice, and tears welled in her eyes. "They would have had to kill her to get the book."

Faedra's heart sank. Jocelyn had lost someone she quite obviously loved, and she knew first hand how that felt. She put a comforting arm around her friend's shoulders.

"I'm so sorry Jocelyn."

"Come, we can do no more here," Faen said urgently. "We need to get to the castle, maybe the king knows something that will help us."

They turned to leave, but Faedra stopped short of the door. She could feel something but didn't understand what it was at first.

"No. Wait," she said and looked all around her. She could feel the amulet heat up under her scarf and moved the scarf aside to see the stone in the center of it glowing brightly.

"What is it, Faedra?" Jocelyn asked.

"I'm not sure," she held the amulet in her hand. "Mum didn't say anything in her letter about the amulet glowing." She looked at her ring, it was not glowing so there was no danger near, but she knew something was wrong, she could sense it. What was it trying to tell her? *Think Faedra, think,* she told herself. She closed her eyes and concentrated hard on the feelings surging through her body, then a window in her mind opened and she could see a vision as clear as day.

"If whoever stole the book had to have killed Elvelynn to get it, wouldn't they have just left her body? Why would they have taken it with them?"

Faen and Jocelyn looked at her in confusion.

"She's still here, I can sense her, and she's still alive."

"Where?" Faen said as he stepped closer to her.

"Hold on," she closed her eyes again and scanned the room in her mind. "There." She pointed over to the corner of the room as she opened her eyes.

They all looked over to where Faedra was pointing, but there was nothing there. Faedra ran over and lowered herself to the floor, her face just fractionally above it. She was trying to look through a crack in the floorboards.

"She's under here," she cried, her heart swelling with hope.

Faen looked for something to pry the floorboard with, and grabbed a poker that was resting up against the fireplace. He ran over to where Faedra was lying on the floor, asked her to move aside, and shoved the poker hard between the boards. He pried it open until he could get his hands under, and pulled the board up. They had not been nailed down, so once the first one was up Jocelyn and Faedra helped lift some more until they had uncovered what the floorboards were hiding.

"Oh, Elvelynn," Jocelyn gasped in horror, putting her hand to her mouth.

The body of an old woman lay crumpled unnaturally in a small hole in the floor. She had her hands tied behind her back, and had been gagged. Her wings had been broken when she had been shoved violently into the tiny space. Her eyes, that were full of pain and fear, looked up at the three of them in desperation.

"Stand back," Faen instructed as he kneeled down and lowered his arms into the hole. He gently moved them under Elvelynn's broken body, and eased her up and out of her tiny prison. He carried her over to a chaise that was positioned next to the fireplace, and after laying her down, removed the bonds from her hands and the gag from her mouth, taking care not to cause her anymore distress. She was barely conscious and mumbling something that was incoherent.

"Who did this to you?" Faen whispered in Elvelynn's ear, but the only reply he got was unintelligible.

"Why isn't she healing?" Faedra asked. "You can all heal just like me, can't you?"

"She has been tortured and poisoned. The poison disables us from using our ability to heal. It makes the torture much more effective," he explained gravely. "This is the work of Redcaps, she would have died fairly soon if you hadn't found her. We need to get her to Bedowen, he is the only person who can help her now. He may be able to find an antidote to the poison. If he can, she will be able to heal herself in time." He scooped Elvelynn up in his arms and carried her through the door. Faedra took one last look around at the chaos in the room before she followed them.

"Jocelyn, take Faedra and wait for me outside the castle," he instructed his sister. "I am going to fly Elvelynn to Bedowen's house, I'll meet you there shortly."

He hovered above the ground for a second, turned, and flew away. Jocelyn took hold of Faedra's arm.

"The castle is this way," she said, pointing in the opposite direction.

"How was the amulet able to tell you that Elvelynn was still alive and where to find her?" Jocelyn asked a few moments later as they wandered down the empty streets.

"I don't know," Faedra answered. "Maybe because the amulet was constructed to be used with the book, and because Elvelynn had been in possession of the book for so long it saw them as one and the same. Other than that I have no explanation. All of this is so new to me, I have to keep pinching myself to make sure I'm still awake."

They carried on through the deserted streets in silence. Faedra knew there was nothing she could say to comfort her friend. People had tried to comfort her with words all the time after her mother had died, but she had wished they would stay silent. Nothing they said ever gave her any comfort, their words just reiterated the fact that she had lost someone she loved, and that person was never coming back.

She prayed that Bedowen would be able to help. Elvelynn had looked like a helpless, sweet old lady, but she knew for the room to have been turned upside down the way it was, she must have put up a good fight.

They walked down streets and around corners for what seemed like most of the afternoon. It was a labyrinth of lanes and alleys, not dissimilar to some she had seen in an old town in Spain that she had visited on holiday once. Eventually they turned a corner, and Faedra found herself once again gaping in awe. The street came to an abrupt end and they were standing on the edge of a huge spacious courtyard. A lavish marble fountain stood in the center. Cascading water was flowing from jugs that were held by statues of fairies, into a basin that had been carved into a marble garden. Ornate stone pillars held up an archway that lined both sides of the courtyard, and even though the once lush vegetation that adorned the courtyard was now brown and lifeless, it was still impressive, even in its starkness.

Further behind the fountain there was an enormous double door. Faedra let her eyes wander above the doorway to admire what was beyond it. An immense castle towered above it, and them. Its walls were made of white stone that she could imagine sparkling in the sunlight like Jocelyn had described, but even though it had lost its luster for the time being, it was still majestic in everyway. She didn't even want to hazard a guess as to how big it was, but it certainly dwarfed the one back home in Norwich. This one had more beautifully spiraling turrets than she cared to count, with a flag swaying in the breeze from each one. A great swath of burgundy material with what she assumed was a royal crest emblazoned in gold, hung from the main balcony of the castle, and she imagined that that must be where the king held court.

"Wow," she mumbled, "you guys don't do anything by halves do you?"

Jocelyn replied with a smile and looked up at the castle too. "It is pretty impressive, is it not? Come we shall wait for Faen by the door."

They walked past the fountain on a floor of mosaic artistry that must have taken eons to create it was so big. When they reached the door Faedra sat down on the ground and leaned back up against the wall. She yawned and let her head fall back to rest against the wall, and closed her eyes. The sun was getting low in the sky, promising the close of another day in a few short hours, and she was beyond tired. Faen was not long in arriving. He made his appearance shortly after they did.

"What did Bedowen say?" Jocelyn asked anxiously as soon as his feet touched the ground.

"He thinks that he can keep her stable until he can find an antidote for the poison, but it might be a while. Unfortunately she cannot help us identify who did this to her and won't be able to in time for us to find the book, and reverse this damage." He looked sourly at the dead vegetation around the courtyard. "We need to go and see the king, and find out if he knows of anything that can help us."

Faedra got to her feet as Faen walked up to the doors and rapped hard on them three times. Slowly the two solid doors that must have been at least twenty feet high opened, allowing the three to walk through before they closed again. They were now standing in another spacious, beautifully landscaped area in front of the castle. At one time it would have been the most elaborate flower garden. Home possibly to every kind of flower that existed, but not now, everything had wilted and died.

They walked up the path that led to the entrance to the castle, up some steps to another set of solid doors, and stood before them. Faen rapped hard three times on these, too and again they slowly opened, allowing them entry. Faedra looked around to see if she could see any security cameras. She didn't expect to see any of course, but it was bugging her that they had just gained entry to a castle without there being any kind of visible security. For goodness' sake, there weren't even any guards around. The place seemed deserted. As they walked through this set of double doors though, all that changed very quickly.

As soon as the doors opened the silence swiftly changed to an inarticulate din that was coming from further down the marble corridor they were now standing in. They walked towards the noise, and it grew louder and louder until Faedra could make out that it was lots of angry, concerned voices. They turned through another set of solid oak doors, which were already open this time, and walked straight into a cavernous room that was crammed with people all talking at once. There were lots of them, nearly filling the sizeable room, and this time they noticed her. Some of them eyed her with scrutiny, others looked at her with confusion, some with concern, and others with a knowing expression. She noticed that some of them looked out of place, too. A distinct feeling of unease swept over her, and she subconsciously moved closer to Faen until she was almost touching him.

The setting sun was streaming in through vast stained glass windows that lined the walls and depicted scenes from nature. Floating chandeliers bobbed about overhead, casting sparkles of light on the inhabitants of the room below them.

Faen pushed his way through the crowd, and as people caught sight of him they parted to either side like a wake made by a speedboat. Some doffed their hats, others acknowledged him with an incline of their heads, but one thing was for sure, Faedra could see he was very well known, and very well respected. Jocelyn subtly guided Faedra into doing the fairy sandwich thing again as they fell in line behind Faen and followed him in single file until they got through the crowd. Once through the hoards of people, they positioned themselves just behind, and to either side of him. Faedra saw the king then for the first time. He was sitting up rigidly on a throne at the other end of the room and they carried on walking until they reached the steps that led up to the throne.

Faen came to a stop and kneeled in front of the king. Jocelyn did some sort of a curtsy, and Faedra tried and failed miserably to do the same. She had never been before royalty before and had no idea of the formalities, but tried her hardest to not insult the king by her lack of etiquette. At least she was giving it her best effort.

"Your Majesty," Faen spoke with respect, and looked up at the king who gestured with his hand for Faen to stand.

Faedra had noticed that the room was now silent. Even though it was fit to bursting with people, you could hear a pin drop.

"Guardian, I knew you would come. I fear my worst nightmare has come to fruition."

"Your Majesty, we found Elvelynn, she lives."

"She lives? But I sent sentinels to her house to see if she was there and they found nothing. Where was she?"

"Ms. Faedra found her," he answered, and gestured a hand in Faedra's direction. "She had been tortured and poisoned, and they had left her under the floorboards to die. She is with Bedowen now."

Faedra thought she may have been mistaken, but she could swear there was just a hint of pride in Faen's voice when he said it.

"Ah, Lillith's daughter, of course," the king said in dulcet tones as he rose and stepped down from his throne.

He was a commanding figure, and moved with grace and assurance. He had the face of authority, and experience seeped from every fiber of his being. She could tell just by looking at him that he was much much older than he appeared. He wore sumptuous robes made of heavy velvet that were forest green in color and edged with the obligatory gold trim. The same crest she had seen on the huge banner draped from the balcony outside, was embroidered onto his robes also. Faedra gulped and gave him a feeble smile as he came to a standstill in front of her. His presence alone was compelling enough to fill the entire hall they were standing in.

The king took Faedra's chin in his hand and moved her face gently from side to side, examining her features with interest. At first Faedra felt incredibly uncomfortable, if not just a little scared, but when she dared herself to look into the king's eyes she saw only sadness there. "You are the image of your mother, my dear child," he spoke in a whisper so that only she could hear. "You cannot even imagine what your being here means to me."

She gave him a puzzled look, but he had already let go of her chin and had turned to stand in front of Faen.

"Come," he said to all three, "I need to speak with you in private." He gestured to a door to the side of the room and walked ahead.

As they made to follow him the room once more erupted into a frenzied hubbub. The people here obviously wanted some answers, and as yet, Faedra doubted that the king had been able to give them any.

They followed the king through an elaborately carved wooden door and into another vast room. The walls were lined from floor to ceiling with bookshelves full of books, an immense library by anyone's standards. Faedra glanced at a few as they followed the king to where he had seated himself behind an imposing oversized desk in the center of the room.

"You have Shakespeare's *A Midsummer Night's Dream*?" she blurted in surprise, without giving a thought to the company she was in. She had just not imagined that the fae king would read Shakespeare. Especially the one about fairies, and wondered what he thought of it. She blushed when she turned to see Faen and Jocelyn looking at her incredulously, and decided it may be wiser not to ask.

"Indeed, my child, I found it very," the king paused, "intriguing. Now, shall we get to the business at hand?"

"Yes, of course," Faedra blustered as she walked over to join them. "Sorry."

"No need my dear. I understand that this is all, shall we say, new to you. You just turned of age yesterday, did you not?"

"Yes, Sir, I did."

He rose and stepped around the desk until he was standing in front of Faedra once more. She had to physically stop herself from taking a step back when he suddenly brought his hands up to her neck. Her eyes widened with concern and were met with a warm smile, which made her relax a little. He untied the scarf and let it hang open around her neck, uncovering the amulet as his did so. She was surprised when he lifted it from her skin and held it in the palm of his hand to examine it. He looked at it with the warm expression you would give a dear friend who you hadn't seen for a while.

"Well, I have to tell you my dear child. You are the first Custodian since I passed the amulet to be hidden in the World of Men, to find themselves in this predicament. There has only been one other Custodian, in all that time, who has ever entered the Land of Azran," he stared deeply into her eyes for a moment. She couldn't quite read the emotion behind his gaze, then he sighed, averted his eyes, and laid the amulet carefully back against her skin. He turned, and resumed his position behind his desk.

"Sire," Faen said as soon as the king was seated, "do you have any idea who may have taken the book?"

The king shook his head. "Unfortunately I do not, Guardian, but the situation is more involved than just the stolen book." He hung his head and took a deep breath as if fighting to keep his composure. "Is the same thing happening in the World of Men as it is here?

"Yes, Sire, it is," Faen replied.

Faedra and Jocelyn listened intently, watching Faen's every gesture and expression as the king continued.

"My daughter, Vivianna, was visiting with Elvelynn at the time of the attack. She was taken, along with the Book of Anohs," he sighed.

"I am so very sorry, Your Majesty," Faen replied.

"There is more," the king continued, and looked gravely over at Faedra, which caused goose bumps to appear on her arms. "They have demanded I hand over the amulet in exchange for my daughter's safe return." He handed Faen a piece of paper with some writing on it that Faedra had never seen before.

"We cannot hand over the amulet, Sire, you know the implications of that. It is not just nature that would die."

"I know that, Guardian. Do not concern yourself, I have no intention of handing over the amulet or…" and he stopped mid sentence and glanced at Faedra.

The hairs on the back of Faedra's neck bristled. She knew exactly what he was about to say. If he had to hand over the amulet, she would still be attached to it. She was the only one who could use it, or she would have to be dead for someone else to.

"You are the best I have, Guardian, I am entrusting you with finding the book and bringing my daughter safely back to me."

"Yes, Sire, you have my word," Faen assured the king.

Faedra couldn't stifle it anymore, and another loud yawn escaped. Three pairs of eyes all turned in unison to look at her, and she could feel her cheeks burn. Here they were talking about the impending doom of goodness knows how many realms, plus the kidnap of a Princess, and she could hardly keep her eyes open.

"I'm sorry," she mumbled through her embarrassment.

"You are tired my child, tonight you will all feast and rest. You will need your energy for the journey ahead." The king clapped his hands and two beautiful fairies appeared at his side. "See to it that they all get plenty to eat and the best rooms in the castle," he commanded. They nodded their understanding and flew to hover either side of the group of three.

Faedra looked at them, and although she admired their staggering beauty and was entranced by the way their wings beat rhythmically to keep them flying, she also realized how quickly she had become accustomed to being surrounded by fae. It dawned on her now that she hardly even noticed their wings anymore. They were as much a natural part of them as their arms or legs were.

"This way please." One of the fairies said in a lilting voice, and gestured towards a different door from the one they had entered through, much to Faedra's relief. She hadn't much liked the idea of having to walk back through the rabble that was waiting for them in the great hall.

"Good luck," the King said as they exited the library room. "If anyone can find the book and return my daughter I know you will be the one to do it."

Faen inclined his head in that gracious way he always did when acknowledging someone, and continued out the door.

CHAPTER TWELVE

They followed in silence behind the two fairies that the king had assigned to them. For the second time since they arrived Faedra noticed that it was only her footsteps that could be heard on the hard marble floor beneath them. She looked over at Jocelyn and then to Faen to see if they were hovering above the floor, but they were not. They were walking just as she was, but they stepped so lightly their footfalls were whisper quiet. It didn't help that she was wearing her riding boots that had fairly hard soles.

She started to feel embarrassed about the way her footsteps reverberated off the walls of the grandly decorated corridor they were walking down, and made a conscious effort to soften her steps. It was not easy, she almost had to walk on tiptoes, and try doing that when you needed to keep up with others who were moving with definite purpose in front of you.

They turned a corner and walked down another corridor. Faedra could feel that Faen was deep in thought, she wasn't quite sure what would be going through Jocelyn's mind, though she had a pretty good idea her friend was wondering how Elvelynn was doing. They carried on down the corridor until it came to its conclusion at another big wooden door. One of the fairies pointed at it and it opened up before they reached it. All three followed the fairies through the door into a vast bustling kitchen.

Yet again Faedra looked around in awe. The kitchen was almost the same size as the great hall they had been in earlier, although the ceilings were not as tall. Down the center of the room stood a long, solid oak table. Faedra guessed that it stretched about thirty feet long by about three feet wide, and along either side of it were lined little people like Todmus, busily preparing food.

Some were rolling dough, some were chopping vegetables. She saw one woman making a pie, and another peeling potatoes. Each of them had a specific task and they were going about it with studious enthusiasm. There must have been at least thirty people working in perfect harmony, making the table its own little industry. She scanned the rest of the room. From the ceiling hung vast cast iron racks from which pots and pans of all shapes and sizes hung. Down one wall of the kitchen there were sinks and draining boards, and a hoard of workers were busily scrubbing pans, drying them, and stacking them in neat piles.

On the opposite side of the room, the wall hosted several huge fireplaces, easily big enough for her to stand up in. A couple of the fireplaces had fires blazing in them with a hog turning on a spit above the flames. A couple of little men bustled about tending to the fires and keeping them hot enough to cook the meat roasting above. Another of the fireplaces did not have an open fire, but was home to an immense cast iron oven, easily ten times the size of the old fashioned stoves she had seen in history books back home.

No one had even given them a second look when they had entered they were so engrossed in their work, and Faedra felt slightly relieved about that. She was feeling more and more like a fish out of water as each moment passed, but the minute she stepped foot into the vast kitchen a feeling of calm swept over her. Even though the kitchen teemed with life, and people were going about their business with an energy that was almost palpable, there was just something about being in a kitchen that brought everyone to the same level.

The fairies motioned for them to follow down to the end of the table. They spoke to a couple of the women working there who looked up to acknowledge the three, nodded their heads, and shuffled themselves and the food they were preparing further down the table to make room at the end. Three chairs appeared out of nowhere, and the fairies gestured to Faen, Faedra and Jocelyn to sit and make themselves comfortable. Faedra noticed that Faen waited for her and Jocelyn to be seated before he sat himself. Within a few moments a couple of the little people walked up and placed plates full of food on the table in front of them.

"Thank you," Faedra spoke to them as they bustled around her, laying an empty plate, cutlery, and a goblet before her. She was responded to with a warm smile and a gracious head bob, just like the one Faen was famous for. They didn't speak but the fact that they gazed intently at the amulet hanging on show around her neck, and then quickly averted their eyes, did not escape her, but it did not make her feel as nervous any more. She had accepted the fact that the amulet was now as much a part of her, than she was of it.

She turned her attention to the plates of food the dwarves had placed in front of them, and recognized a rumbling deep from within her stomach. She was starving. There was a plump, steaming hot chicken in the middle, surrounded by dishes of steaming, brightly colored vegetables. A dwarf with a pitcher made his way round to all three of them, filling their goblets to the brim. He lingered next to Faedra, shooting a quick glance at the amulet before scuttling off into the pantry again.

Faen gestured for Faedra and Jocelyn to help themselves to the food first.

Ever the gentleman, Faedra thought as she gave him a warm smile and leaned in to pull a leg from the chicken. Dark meat was definitely her favorite. She scooped some vegetables onto her plate and tucked in.

"Do you have any idea where we go from here?" Faedra asked Faen between mouthfuls.

"Tomorrow we journey into the pine forest to summon Kernunnos," he replied, after careful thought.

"How will Kernunnos be able to help, Brother?" Jocelyn asked with interest.

"Um, would someone care to enlighten me as to who Kernunnos is?" Faedra asked, slightly disgruntled. She only started learning about this stuff yesterday, and although she understood that she was at the bottom of an extremely steep learning curve, it irked her how everyone talked as if she already knew what they were talking about. Most of the time she felt horribly in the dark, and didn't like that feeling at all.

"Kernunnos is Lord of the Woods," Faen stated, before turning back to Jocelyn to answer her question. "My dear Jocelyn, I believe Kernunnos can help us because he is closer to nature than any other entity in our realm. Because of what the book controls, he may be able to sense its whereabouts through nature here or in other realms. I am hoping he can point us in the right direction. At the moment it is the only hope I have to start looking for the book."

A thought suddenly occurred to Faedra. All color drained from her face and she had trouble swallowing the food in her mouth. Jocelyn noticed her sudden change of demeanor, and her look turned to one of concern. Faen noticed the unsettled glance that Jocelyn was focusing across the table and turned to see what had caused such a rapid change in her expression. Faedra's face was as white as snow and she was looking blankly into space.

"Whatever is the matter, Faedra?" Jocelyn asked.

Faedra brought her focus back and looked at Faen. "Dad thinks I've gone riding. I've been gone all day, and now it's nighttime. He'll be worried sick, he has no idea where I am." She spoke with fear and desperation in her voice. It was breaking her heart to think of her dad panicking over her disappearance, and there was no way to let him know she was safe, cell phones didn't work between realms.

"Do not worry, Ms. Faedra," Faen responded reassuringly, "your father will not know you are missing. The time in Azran ticks differently than in the World of Men, we can spend much more time here if needs be and you will still have only been gone a few hours."

"Are you sure?" she asked, not quite being able to believe what he was telling her, and imagining her father's panic stricken face on the phone to the Police.

He smiled warmly. He knew the great lengths she had gone to over the years to prevent giving her father any cause to worry about her. A quality he admired and respected. She cared more about those she loved than she did about herself.

"I am sure," he replied. "Your father is blissfully unaware of your whereabouts and I will make sure it stays that way. We will return to the World of Men in plenty of time before he would start to wonder where you have got to."

She heaved a sigh of relief and the color returned to her face.

"Thank you," she whispered.

He inclined his head.

After they had finished their meal, the two fairies appeared.

"We have prepared your rooms for you." they sang in unison, and gestured for the three to follow. They all got up and continued behind them. Faedra was looking forward to being able to flop onto a bed and finally get some sleep. She was exhausted, and imagined that what she was feeling must be similar to jet lag. She had never been on a long haul flight, but her friends had, and how they had explained it to her, it had sounded just like she felt.

They followed the fairies up umpteen spiraling stairs, along what seemed like miles of corridors until they eventually stopped, and the fairies pointed to three doors that were adjacent to each other.

"You will find everything you need to make your stay comfortable," they sang. "If you find you need anything further, you only have to ask and one of us will attend to your needs directly."

"Thank you," Faen, Faedra and Jocelyn replied together.

The fairies disappeared around a corner, and they were alone in the corridor.

"Well goodnight," Faedra said.

"Goodnight, Ms. Faedra."

"Goodnight, Faedra."

Jocelyn and Faen exchanged their goodnights, and they all entered their rooms in synchronization, as if the move had been choreographed. Faedra closed the door behind her, leaned back up against it and sucked in a sharp breath.

"Oh wow!" she breathed as she scanned the room that sprawled out in front of her.

It was easily the size of the entire ground floor of her house, and was furnished with the finest ornate, elaborately detailed furniture that she had ever laid her eyes on. At one end of the room an immense marble fireplace took center stage, filling nearly the entire wall, and was complete with a blazing fire crackling happily within it. A deep burgundy chaise trimmed with gold, sat in front of the fire just waiting to invite someone to sit there.

Wood paneling stretched all the way around the room to about half way up the walls. Above it rich wallpaper lined the walls, and elaborate gold sconces with opaque glass lampshades protruded, a soft glow emanating from each one. She looked above her as she now noticed she was drenched in a soft light. A small chandelier bobbed above her head, showering her with soft sparkling light. She stepped to the side, it followed. She stepped forward, it followed.

"No way," she gasped, as she realized where she went, so did the chandelier, lighting a path for her every step of the way.

On the other side of the room was a four-poster bed that she imagined to be the size of her entire bedroom. It was made of a rich mahogany and the posts were carved with intricate spirals. It had sumptuous, velvet burgundy drapes the same color as the chaise, and a gold satin comforter covered the bed. She wandered over to it and ran her fingers along the heavy velvet material, and then onto the soft satin comforter.

A pair of cream silk pajamas had been laid out for her on the bed, and she held them up to her to determine if they were the right size, they were. She smiled, why ever would she have thought otherwise? She wandered past the bed to a pair of glass doors that stood the height of the wall, at least ten feet tall. They were framed in gold with gold handles. She opened them and walked through onto the balcony where they led. She looked down to one side and saw the city below that was lit only by the silvery light of the moon, casting its eerie light on the buildings it watched over. She looked in the other direction and could see the valley stretch out until it met with a mountain range that loomed majestically in the distance. She wondered in which direction they would travel tomorrow to reach the pine forest.

A shiver ran through her and she walked back inside. There was a chill in the air and she was only wearing a t-shirt and jeans. The doorway next to the glass doors led to a lavish bathroom. Mirrors lined one entire wall, the rest of the room was made out of marble, and accessorized with gold fittings. Steam rose from the water filling a sunken bath that had quite obviously been run for her. Fluffy towels were stacked in a neat pile next to the bath, and a toothbrush had been placed next to one of the two basins. They weren't kidding, they had certainly thought of everything to make her feel comfortable. She undressed and slid into the warm water. A sigh of epic proportions escaped as she submerged herself up to her neck.

Once she had bathed she dried herself, and with a towel wrapped around her torso, wandered back to the bedroom and dressed into her pajamas, laying her clothing neatly over the back of a chair that was placed next to the bed. She had to wear them again the next day so she made an effort not to get them too crumpled. She lifted the covers and slid between the sheets that felt like pure silk. The sconces turned themselves off, and the chandelier above her head dimmed to blackness.

She sat up with a start. "No, please do go out completely," she said with an urgency that surprised even her. She'd never been scared of the dark before and cursed the Redcap for making her feel this way. For a split second she wondered who she was kidding, the lights weren't intelligent they wouldn't respond to a spoken request, but all the lights came back on in an instant, and then dimmed to a soft glow.

"Thank you," she spoke to the room as whole, and lay her head back down on the pillow.

Unfortunately, instead of falling asleep as soon as her head touched it, she was wide-awake. She lay motionless for a few minutes with her eyes closed trying to will herself to sleep. She moved to one side then to the other. Nothing, she was still wide-awake. After about an hour of tossing and turning she threw back the covers and sat up in exasperation.

This is not fair, she thought, *why can't I sleep? I'm so tired.* She went through a list of possibilities. The bed was comfortable, that wasn't it. It wasn't dark, that wasn't it either, then it dawned on her and a light bulb came on above her head and it wasn't the chandelier. She had not slept on her own since she was six years old. Faen had always been right there sleeping on the rug beside her bed, every night for more than eleven years.

She turned, hung her legs over the edge of the mattress and slid her feet into the slippers that had been left for her beside the bed. She made her way through the door and wandered down the corridor. She tapped quietly on Faen's door as she opened it, and poked her head through the opening she had just created. It was dark inside, no sound of movement.

"Faen?" she whispered as she entered the room, and clicked the door shut behind her. "Faen?" she whispered again.

She heard a rustle coming from her left, and turned her head just as a soft light appeared over Faen's head as he sat up in bed.

She noticed he did not have a shirt on and there was a catch in her breath as she let her eyes scan his perfectly formed torso. He noticed her gaze and looked down at himself. Almost instantaneously, he materialized a soft cotton shirt from nowhere to cover his chest. He looked back up at Faedra who was standing over by the door looking rather uncomfortable.

"Ms. Faedra? Is something the matter?" Faen asked in response to the look of sadness on her face. His features were soft, his expression welcoming, and his hair mussed. He ran a hand through it to try and smooth it down.

He had such a presence here in his home, somehow different to when he was in her home, and Faedra wondered if he felt as much of a fish out of water in her world, as she did in his. She took a hesitant step forward. She was eighteen now, an adult. Not to mention Custodian to a very powerful fae element, and her brain was telling her she should feel silly not being able to sleep without her dog, but the dreadfully lonely sensation welling within her was overwhelming. She swallowed hard and looked down at her feet. *He's going to think me stupid and childish.*

"Ms. Faedra, whatever is the matter?" he asked again.

"I, um, I'm so tired, but I can't sleep," her voice cracked with emotion, "then I realized why," she looked up at him, tears pricking behind her eyes.

"Why?" he prompted.

"Because for more than eleven years now you have slept beside me and I… err… miss you."

His expression changed to one of compassion that Faedra had not seen on his face before, but had seen in the eyes of her dog many times. He patted the bed beside him.

"Come," he simply said.

She breathed in with relief. She hadn't realized until that point that she'd been holding her breath. She moved swiftly to his bed and climbed up to sit crossed legged to the side of him.

"Would you like me or your dog?"

The question took her by surprise. She thought about it for a second. "You, please," she whispered, and smiled at him sheepishly.

Faen returned her smile with a warm one of his own that he didn't hand out very often.

"Very well then, I shall stay," he said with an incline of his head.

The soft glow of the light above illuminated just the two of them in the immense bedroom. Everything else was shrouded in darkness. Faedra leaned forward and carefully picked up the talisman hanging around his neck. She noticed a catch in his breath as her fingers brushed against his skin, and brought her gaze up to meet his. His eyes were liquid pools of aqua full of emotion, and they locked onto hers, not letting them go.

After a silent moment she managed to tear her gaze from his and looked at the talisman she had laid in the palm of her hand, moving it under the light. She had noticed it before, but had never really looked at it closely. It was round, and looked like it was made of ivory, although it had an iridescent quality to it that she had not seen in ivory before. A leather thong threaded through a hole at the top held it around Faen's neck. The center of the talisman was carved with a beautiful Celtic design, and a band around the outer edge had lots of symbols carved into it.

"This is beautiful. What is it made of?"

"The horn of a Unicorn."

"Wow, really?" she shook her head in amazement as he nodded. "I recognize these symbols, but I can't think where from."

"They are runes. You probably saw them when you were at the festival."

She nodded her head. That was where she had seen them before, when Rose had seen something of her destiny in them, but refused to tell her what. "Of Course." She lay the talisman gently back against his skin.

"Can I ask you a question?" she said.

"Of course," he replied.

"Are you immortal?"

Faen chuckled at her question. "No, Ms. Faedra, I am not. Although, fae do live much longer than humans, so that is where the myth probably stems from. We die of old age just like you do. We can be killed, but not very easily, and not by human hands." Then he thought about his last comment and rephrased it. "I should say, not by human hands, present company excluded."

Faedra's eyebrows shot up. "You mean I can kill a fairy? Not that I would want to of course," she added hastily.

"Well, there is no point having a power if it does not protect you and the amulet against the very creatures who are likely to come after you to get it."

"Good point," she agreed. "So how old are you then?"

He raised an eyebrow. "You said a question, Ms. Faedra."

"Oh come on, Faen, you know me inside and out, and I hardly know anything about you. Apart from what dog food you prefer and that you like to be scratched behind your ears," she gave him a wry smirk.

He conceded. "Very well, you may ask me some more questions, what do you wish to know?"

"Your age?"

"Oh yes, hmm let me see now. We age much slower than humans do, about ten times slower I believe, so that would make me about two hundred and three of your years."

"No way!" Faedra exclaimed. "You only look about twenty."

He smiled.

"So how long do you live then, bearing in mind that you don't get killed by a rogue Custodian?"

"Oh, about a thousand of your years give or take a few," he smiled again.

Faedra gaped at him in disbelief and he nodded his head to reiterate his statement. She shuffled up the bed and turned to lie down on top of the covers next to where he was sitting. She looked up at the soft glowing ball of light that was bobbing gracefully above them.

"Tell me about my mother," she shifted her attention from the light to Faen's face.

His smile faded and sadness filled his eyes. "What do you wish to know?"

"Well I was only six when she died, and it was so long ago that I can't remember too much about her and I get scared that given a few more years I will forget everything about her."

"I didn't actually know your mother very well," he started. "I was only assigned to her a few months before she was killed." He dropped his eyes and Faedra could tell he still carried much regret over what had happened. "What I did know of her was that she was a very caring woman. She loved all living things and adored the ground you walked on. She would have gone to the ends of the earth for you, Faedra, she loved you that much."

"She was also very dedicated to her role as Custodian and took it very seriously. She had spent many years training in the sword skills, and as I said, she was one of the best sword fighters I have ever seen. I know for a fact she would have been very proud of how you have grown and matured. You have taken to being Custodian very much in your stride, a natural she would have said. She was a natural, very capable of looking after herself, as I said before I was only assigned to her so that she could teach me, and I failed her." He looked with determination into Faedra's captivated eyes. "I will not make the same mistake twice."

Faedra gave him a knowing smile. "Thank you."

"You are very welcome."

"Faen?"

"Yes."

"You have to stop blaming yourself for my mum's death. It wasn't your fault. I don't blame you, I blame the Redcaps, and one day I will have my revenge on them."

He gave her a weak smile, and Faedra sensed that he wasn't about to stop blaming himself for the death of her mother, but in time she would convince him that he was not to blame. A loud yawn escaped before she could stifle it, and her eyes grew so heavy she was fighting to keep them open.

"Ms. Faedra, you are very tired, you need to sleep."

"I know, but I don't want to go back into that big empty room…" She was asleep before she finished her sentence.

Faen looked at her for a long moment and sighed a contented sigh. He brushed the back of his fingers over her cheek then leaned over and grabbed some of the excess piece of comforter that hung over the edge of the bed, wrapping it around her. He lay down beside her watching her breathing steadily in and out for a few minutes as she slept soundly next to him. Then he couldn't help himself, he wrapped a protective arm around her before he fell asleep with her safely tucked up against him. Making sure to leave the soft light glowing above them incase she woke up in the night. She didn't.

CHAPTER THIRTEEN

Faedra opened her eyes and stretched. She couldn't remember sleeping that well for a very long time. She turned her head to see Faen looking at her. He was lying on his side, propping his head up on his arm.

"Good morning, Ms. Faedra," he greeted her with a warm smile, "I trust you slept well."

"Morning, Faen, yes I did thank you," she answered, returning his smile with one of her own.

"Well we better get moving, we have another long day ahead of us today," he pushed his covers back and gracefully slid off the bed.

Faedra was still lying on top of the covers. She looked down at the excess piece of comforter that she had been cocooned in, and peeled it back. She smiled, he had allowed her to fall asleep next to him and had made sure she didn't get cold. The sound of water running from the bathroom caught her attention. She better get a move on and go back to her room to wash her face and get dressed.

"I'm going back to my room to get changed," she called as she slid off the bed.

Faen poked his head around the bathroom door, he was brushing his teeth. Faedra couldn't help herself, she laughed.

He frowned, he couldn't speak his mouth was full of toothbrush.

"I'm sorry," she chuckled. "I had just never pictured that fairies brushed their teeth, or needed to do any of the mundane personal grooming that us humans have to, for that matter."

He smiled around his toothbrush and shrugged his shoulders.

"Meet you out in the corridor in a few minutes?"

He nodded and disappeared back into the bathroom.

When she arrived back in her room she noticed that the bed had been made and her clothes were neatly laid out on it. They had been cleaned and pressed, and her boots polished and set beside the bed. She quickly changed then went into the bathroom to do the mundane personal grooming that humans do. Several minutes later she headed out the door. Faen and Jocelyn were already waiting there for her.

"Morning, Jocelyn, did you sleep well?" she asked.

"Yes thank you, Faedra, and you?"

Faedra glanced at Faen who was watching her intently. They exchanged a subtle smile. "Yes, thank you, I did," she responded.

"Come," Faen said with a sweeping motion of his arm in the direction of the kitchen. "We must eat first, and then begin our journey to the pine forest."

Luckily Faen seemed to know where he was going because without a doubt Faedra would have gotten herself hopelessly lost in the maze of corridors in this seemingly endless castle. After a while they made it to the kitchen, and Faedra was ravenous again. She had noticed her appetite had increased substantially since she acquired her power, but she hadn't used it for more than a day now and was wondering if it was normal for her to be eating as much as she was. Maybe it was still residual energy conservation from when she had had to use her power to fight off a Redcap.

They ate a hearty breakfast and were each given a knapsack full of food, and an oilskin pouch full of water, which they slung across their bodies. They made their way through the castle to the main entrance. Faen rapped hard on the door again and it swung open gracefully. They walked through it and were greeted by a handsome fairy in uniform.

"The king has given you these horses," he told them, holding out his hand in the direction of where three beautiful horses stood. They were black as midnight with thick silver manes and tails that shimmered in the sunlight. Faedra was speechless, she had never seen such stunning creatures. Their immaculate coats shone with a luster not from her world. One of them snorted and pawed at the ground.

"I'll take him," she said as she walked past Faen and Jocelyn. She had no doubt in her mind that she was about to have the ride of her life. Faen raised his eyebrows in surprise.

"What? You think I can't handle him, don't you?"

"On the contrary, Ms. Faedra, I have seen you ride. I have no doubt that you are perfectly capable of handling that stallion," he replied.

"What is it then?" she asked, narrowing her eyes at him.

"It is nothing, Ms. Faedra." Truth was, he was starting to see the little girl he'd watched growing up, turn into a tenacious young woman with just a hint of vulnerability about her, and he thought that she every bit deserved the title of Custodian. If he didn't know any better he would imagine that it was pride seeping from his every pore right at that moment.

The uniformed fairy gave Faedra a leg up, and as soon as she was on the horse's back he reared, then came back to the ground and pawed again. Faedra felt an electric excitement surging through her as she felt the intense energy of the beautiful beast she was sitting on.

"Come on you two, what are you waiting for, we have a Lord of the Woods to find."

Faen and Jocelyn glanced at each other with a look that said 'oh dear what have we unleashed'. They mounted their horses, and all three galloped off through the courtyard, out of the city, and headed in the direction of the pine forest.

They rode for hours across the dying landscape, and although Faedra was saddened by the devastation around her, she had never felt this alive before. The horse beneath her was a powerhouse of muscle and speed, and they flew like the wind. Her legs didn't turn to jelly this time, instead she embraced the power she was feeling from the magnificent beast she was riding. To the point she could feel her whole body was tingling with electric energy.

After a few hours of riding Faedra could see a browning forest loom up ahead, and they all slowed down to a trot and gradually a walk. They came to a stop at the edge of the forest and gave the trees a long hard look.

"Oh, Brother, even the evergreens are dying," Jocelyn's voice rang with sadness as they all looked down at the thick carpet of brown pine needles that had fallen from the dying trees.

"We will find the book, Jocelyn, we will reverse this," Faen promised her, his voice sounding almost as sad as his little sister's. "Come, we must find Kernunnos."

He moved his horse forward. Faedra and Jocelyn fell into line behind him as they all entered the forest.

Faedra found the forest eerie, and after a while she realized why. There were no sounds of life here. No birds were singing in the trees, no wildlife scuttling about on the ground, or squirrels chasing each other along the limbs, jumping from one tree to the next. There was nothing, just an unearthly silence except for the soft hoof falls the horses were making as they ventured deeper and deeper into the forest.

They followed Faen for about another hour until they came across an opening between the trees in the heart of the forest. They stood on the edge of the clearing for a moment. It was almost a perfect circle, and right in the center stood an ancient, gnarly pine tree, much taller and wider than any pine tree Faedra had ever seen.

They dismounted and left the horses. Faedra wondered if they should tie them up but Faen assured her they would not go anywhere. He told her the horses were 'assigned' to them and would not leave until they were permitted to. She wished Gypsy were so obedient, thinking back to that day in the woods when her horse left her there without so much as backwards glance.

Faedra and Jocelyn followed behind Faen as they cautiously made their way towards the huge pine taking center stage in the clearing. He stopped about ten feet away from it, closed his eyes, and held his hands out, palms facing upwards, and started chanting.

"Open glade in dark wood,
fertile tree in clearing stood.
Lord of the Woods, your help we need,
respect and honor, ours to heed.
Appear to us, this we plea,
Kernunnos hear, we summon thee."

Faedra held her breath. Nothing happened. "Was something supposed to happen?" she leaned over and whispered to Jocelyn.

Jocelyn shrugged her shoulders. "I do not know, I have never seen an invocation before," she admitted.

"Quiet," Faen turned his head and snapped at them. "This will only work in absolute silence." Faedra mouthed a sorry to him and closed her lips tight.

Faen repeated the invocation again, a little louder this time and with a lot more passion. Still nothing, but Faedra kept her mouth shut this time and just looked all around her, having absolutely no idea what to expect.

Again Faen repeated the invocation, with yet more emphasis and passion. This time it worked and Faedra realized at that point that she had watched *The Wizard of Oz* far too many times. She had been expecting the tree to grow limbs that looked like arms, and a big gnarly face to appear in the bark of the trunk and start shouting at them, but that couldn't have been further from what actually did happen.

It suddenly grew darker, not a pitch black dark, but a setting sun through the trees kind of dark, causing an ethereal glow to cloak the clearing. A mist appeared from the trees surrounding the clearing. It smelled strongly of a musky essential oil that she recognized as being patchouli, and crept low to the ground in tendril like wisps until it had filled the entire space. Faedra scanned the perimeter of the clearing, but could see nothing but the mist encircling them. Her attention turned back to the ancient tree in the center when she heard a creaking sound that seemed to be coming from within. An opening appeared in the bark, narrow at first but then expanding into an archway, from which an incredibly self-assured looking man walked, with a stunning white stag at his side.

Faedra swallowed hard. She didn't know what she was expecting the Lord of the Woods to look like, but the man walking towards them now was definitely not it. He glided with ethereal grace to stand in front of Faen, who kneeled before him. He was tall with dark brown, shoulder length hair and neatly trimmed beard flecked with gray, dark olive skin, and deep forest green eyes. He looked wise beyond his years, and Faedra didn't even want to hazard a guess as to how old he actually was.

He wore robes that flowed around him with a fluidity that reminded Faedra of when she used to watch the rock pools at the beach. Every time a wave would come and recede away again, it would leave the water in the rock pool swirling around until the next time. His robes were colored with the various hues of woodland, including russet, deep forest green, and autumn gold.

"Rise, Guardian," he commanded, and Faen did as he asked. "You summoned me?"

"I did, My Lord," Faen responded, and bowed his head with respect. "Someone has stolen the Book of Anohs and we need to find it before whoever it is destroys our realm and the World of Men, and possibly many other realms, too."

"And how do you think that I may help, Guardian?" Kernunnos asked.

"I believe that because the book controls nature, and you are in essence, Lord over an immense part of nature, I was hoping you may be able to sense where the book is located."

"Hmm," Kernunnos rubbed his chin and walked over to Faedra, who gulped again. "And you, my child are not from this realm," he caught sight of the amulet. "Ah, a Custodian, well now I understand why you stand before me."

Faedra swallowed hard. The King of Azran didn't hold a torch to the presence that Kernunnos exuded. He finished scrutinizing Faedra and walked back to stand before Faen. Then he closed his eyes and held his arms outstretched. He stood there in silence for a few moments, and when he opened his eyes again they were completely white, no eyeball, nothing, just white. Faedra took a step back as she sucked in a breath and covered her mouth with her hand.

"I see giant white horses several hundred feet tall, a hill that is perfectly round, near a spire so high it touches the sky. A circle of stone surrounded by A's, is where the book can be found." He closed his eyes, and when he opened them again they had returned to their normal color.

"But what does that mean?" Faen asked, confused by the cryptic clue.

"I can only tell you what I see, Guardian, my powers do not give me a road map."

"Do you know in which realm we may start to look?"

"I do not. I am sorry I cannot give you clearer directions."

"Thank you, My Lord, you have at least given us something to work with," Faen bowed his head.

"Good luck, Guardian," Kernunnos said as he turned toward the tree. Then he paused, turned back to look at Faedra, and inclined his head.

"Custodian," he acknowledged, before continuing to walk back into the tree.

As soon as the archway in the tree sealed up behind Kernunnos and his stag, the mist cleared and the sunlight once again rained down upon them.

Faen scratched his head. "I was hoping for more precise direction than that," he said. "There are no horses that large in any realm."

"Horses, horses," Faedra mumbled to herself, pacing back and forth as she meandered closer and closer to the edge of the clearing. She was holding her chin in her hand, her brow furrowed. "Surrounded by a's? Why does that sound so familiar?" she continued her pacing for a few more moments, mumbling under her breath trying to connect the pieces of information to something buried deep in her memory.

"Oh my God!" Faedra blurted. The others turned to look at her stunned expression. "I think I know where it is."

"Where, Ms. Faedra?" Faen asked urgently as he and Jocelyn walked over to where she was pacing.

"I'll take you there. It's in my world," she said with excitement.

"No, it is too dangerous. Tell me where it is, and I will go," Faen insisted.

"Like heck you will. I'm going with you."

"No, you are not," Faen raised his voice. He didn't do that very often.

"Yes, I am," Faedra shot him a warning glare.

"No, Ms. Faedra, you are not."

"Yes… I… Am!"

Jocelyn sighed and sat herself down on a nearby boulder. She could see this was going to take a while. She watched the argument unfold before her, moving her head from Faen to Faedra as if watching a tennis match.

"You are making me angry," Faedra growled several minutes into their back and forth battle. With a glare that could kill, she opened up her palms to reveal two glowing orbs of blue.

Faen looked down at her hands and scoffed. "You would never use them on me," he said, with a look that oozed arrogance.

Who was she kidding? Of course she wouldn't, and she threw them at a nearby tree where they exploded on impact, shattering the bark, and sending fragments of wood showering over Jocelyn.

"Sorry, Jocelyn," she called as she noticed her friend sweeping bits of bark off her dress, and picking it out of her hair. Then she turned on Jocelyn's brother again. "I do not need to be wasting my energy on you, either," she scowled at him.

"You'll upset Kernunnos," he goaded as he looked over at the splintered tree.

She glared at him again and balled her hands into fists, and rested them on her hips, squaring her shoulders as she did. She lifted her chin in defiance, and they stood in silence for a while, a frosty stand off that neither was willing to concede to.

Eventually Jocelyn broke the angry silence.

"Um, you two, the fate of all realms rests with you, and all that," she said with concern. They turned together and glared at her. She put her hands up "Okay, Okay, just thought I would mention it."

They went back to glaring uncompromisingly at each other, and a few more moments passed.

"Sometimes, Ms. Faedra, you can be impossibly stubborn," Faen spoke first.

Faedra raised an eyebrow at him. "And sometimes, MR. Faen, you can be impossibly arrogant," she snapped back at him.

They continued staring at each other. Then Faedra noticed a subtle shift in the way Faen was looking at her. The frustrated expression he was wearing melted away and was replaced by one of consideration. He leaned in and cupped her face. Before her brain even had time to react, he had planted his lips very self-assuredly on hers, which sent a tingle of electricity throughout her face, down her neck and along her spine. Her eyes widened with surprise, and she found she couldn't move. She was frozen to the spot, but her senses were heightened to the point that they were almost crackling with their intensity.

Then she surprised herself. She accepted his kiss and kissed him back. Her hands that had been balled into fists just seconds ago were now tangling themselves through his silken hair. After a moment he pulled away, but still held her face in his hands, and a wry smile curved the corner of his mouth.

"Very well, Faedra," he made sure to exaggerate her name as he inclined his head, "you may come with us," he whispered. His face was still so close to hers she could feel his warm breath on her face as he spoke.

In that instant their paradigm shifted. She was no longer his charge, he no longer her Guardian, although she could sense he would always be her protector. They were now partners with one goal. To retrieve the Book of Anohs and return Vivianna, the king's daughter, safely back to Azran and her father.

"Yay," Jocelyn cried, clapping her hands excitedly, pulling Faen and Faedra from their reverie. They both turned to look at her.

Faen looked at his sister with a puzzled expression, pulling his eyebrows together.

"Well it is about time, Brother," she stated.

He looked back at Faedra who was still reeling from their kiss. They looked at each other and chuckled. Jocelyn stepped down off the boulder, walked over to them and put an arm around each of them.

"Well, now we finally have that out of the way, I assume we need to make our way back to the portal," she said with a smirk.

Faen looked up at the sky, the sun was sinking and it wouldn't be long before darkness enveloped the land again.

"We will make camp here for tonight, it will be dark soon, and not all of Azran is safe to travel at night," he explained. "We will leave at first light."

"Come on, Faedra," Jocelyn said as she took hold of Faedra's arm, "let us go and find some firewood." They headed into the trees.

"Do not go out of sight of the clearing," Faen called out to them in a protective, big brotherly way.

"We won't," Jocelyn called back.

They didn't need to go but a few feet in, as there were plenty of small branches and kindling lying all around them. They bent down and scooped up sticks, holding them in their arms as they did so.

"I guess you were right about the 'wings' thing," Faedra mentioned after they had been searching for a few minutes.

Jocelyn smiled warmly. "I know my brother better than he would like to think I do," she said.

"He still hides them though," Faedra sighed.

"Give him time, Faedra. He has never felt about anyone the way he feels about you, and he didn't even realize that until a few minutes ago."

Faedra looked through the trees into the clearing where Faen was collecting rocks to make a small fire pit. "Neither did I," she whispered under her breath.

"It will be worth the wait, Faedra, his wings are the most spectacular that I have ever seen. If you think mine are beautiful, they do not even come close to my brother's."

Faedra smiled weakly at her friend. "I think we have enough don't we?" she said, holding out her arms that were now full of sticks and small branches.

Jocelyn looked at Faedra's bundle and then at her own. "I think so."

They headed back to the clearing and dropped the wood next to where Faen was placing rocks in a neat circle. He was being extra careful to make sure that the fire could not spread. Everything surrounding them was so tinder dry the whole lot could catch fire very easily.

The sun sank beyond the horizon, and darkness replaced it. They grabbed the rolled up bedding that had been attached the back of each saddle - the king had thought of everything – and unrolled their 'beds' around the campfire that Faen had started with a click of his fingers. They sat down beside the warming flames that licked up into the night, occasionally sending sparks up into the sky when a knot in a piece of wood crackled and popped.

Faedra sat peacefully while Faen and Jocelyn spoke in hushed voices to each other. She was trying to see if she could control her energy without the emotion of anger. So far that had been the only time she had been able to use it, when she was angry.

The first time she had used it, she was feeling anger and frustration at not being able to materialize anything, then wham, there it was. The next time, her fear had changed to anger behind the hotel when she had imagined her dad finding her dead on the cold floor. Her power had surged through her uncontrollably that time. Then a little while ago she had been getting angry with Faen but was not angry enough that she hadn't been able to control it.

She had tuned Jocelyn and Faen out now. She didn't know what they were talking about, sibling stuff she assumed. She was going to get a grip on her power if it was the last thing she did. She closed her eyes and imagined the sensations that flowed through her body when the energy manifested itself, and she tried to recreate that feeling. She wanted to be able to rely on using her power if she needed to, when they met whoever was in possession of the book. She wanted the ability to use it in a skillful way, and not just as a knee jerk reaction.

It took a few times, but after some serious concentration, there it was. She could feel a warm sensation in her hands and she opened her eyes to see two balls of blue light bobbing gracefully just above her skin. The reflection in her eyes from the sparkling energy made them look like they were twinkling in the darkness. She smiled and closed her palms, pushing the sensation back. She opened her palms again and the light was gone.

She tried this several more times, and each time she felt more and more in control of the energy coursing through her body. She was elated, and stared in awe for a few moments at the balls of energy bobbing above her hands. It was mesmerizing, almost hypnotic. A warm feeling surrounded her hands and they closed, but she hadn't closed them herself. She looked up to see Faen kneeling in front of her, his hands wrapped around hers, and she gave him a quizzical look.

"I have been watching you control your power for a while now. You are learning quickly, but you do not have much food and will burn yourself out."

She could hear the concern in his voice, and gave him a warm smile. His face glowed in the soft light from the fire.

"You're right," she said. Until he had stopped her, she hadn't noticed how hungry she was getting. She leaned over to get her knapsack and opened it up, retrieved half of its contents, and started eating. She knew how weak she would feel if she didn't eat quickly.

She looked over to Jocelyn who was now sleeping soundly beside the fire. How long had she been doing this, and how long had Faen been sitting watching her?

"It's a beautiful night," Faedra said as she looked up to admire the enormous full moon that was pouring its silvery light all over them.

"It is," Faen agreed. He looked over at Jocelyn sleeping. "We must rest if we are to make an early start in the morning." He pulled his bedding over, laid it down next to

Faedra's, and sat down on it. "I will be right here if you need me."

She returned his smile with one of her own and settled down to sleep.

CHAPTER FOURTEEN

Faen knelt down beside Faedra and gently shook her arm. He and Jocelyn had prepared the horses and were ready to leave, but he wanted her to sleep as long as she could. Her eyes cracked open and a smile crept across her lips at the sight of him. She sat up and after stretching her arms upwards, rubbed the sleep from her eyes. She looked for Jocelyn and saw her over by the horses, their things already packed and attached to the saddle, and her smile fell from her face.

"Why didn't you wake me earlier?" she asked in dismay. "Faen, I am always a step behind you guys, and that makes me feel inadequate." Her voice was laced with a tinge of annoyance and embarrassment.

"You needed to sleep as long as possible, Faedra, you used up a lot of your energy last night," he stroked her cheek with the back of his hand, his expression one of concern. "I shouldn't have let you, but you were really starting to understand your power and control it, and you may well need to use it today. It will take but a few moments for us to get you packed and ready."

"Okay," she sighed. He made perfect sense, using her power drained her beyond belief. "I'll let you off this time," she said with a smirk.

The sun was not yet up, but the sky was glowing with that beautiful light that welcomes the day just before the sun decides to peek over the horizon and has every hue of pastel you can imagine. She rubbed her hands over her face, willing herself awake, and accepted Faen's offered hand to help her up off the ground. He hastily rolled her bedding up and carried it over to her horse. She followed.

"Good Morning, Faedra," Jocelyn sang as they approached.

"Morning, Jocelyn."

"Forgive me for saying this, but you don not look too good this morning."

"No forgiveness needed, I don't feel too good either." She imagined how her reflection had looked in the mirror after the first time she had been trying to use her power. She could envision that her skin must be looking pretty pallid right now, with dark circles framing her eyes. That was exactly how she felt, like something was sucking the life out of her. Having a power like hers certainly had its downside.

Faen dug around in her knapsack and held out the rest of her food for her. "Here eat this you will feel better. He dug in his knapsack, too. "Then eat this, you used more of your energy than I realized. When we get through the portal you need a proper meal." He looked concerned, so she tried giving him her 'I'm fine really' look. It didn't work.

She ate while he tied her bedding to the back of the saddle. Jocelyn mounted her horse, and when Faedra had finished her food, Faen gave her a leg up onto hers. She leaned down to adjust her foot in the stirrup, which brought her face level with his.

"Just for the record," he whispered, "you are far from inadequate, in every way."

"Thank you," she whispered back and gave him a sheepish smile. She was starting to feel better already. The food was taking effect, but she knew the small amount she had eaten wouldn't be enough to sustain her for very long. "How far is it to the portal?" she asked.

"About two hours east of here," Faen replied.

"We best get going then" she said, and followed behind Faen as he moved his horse forward. Jocelyn fell in behind Faedra, and she realized she was a fairy sandwich once again.

After about an hour of riding Faedra began to feel decidedly weaker. Why did she have to use that much energy last night? That was stupid when she knew there was nothing much to eat to replace it. The truth was, she wasn't thinking. Her power was so new to her, and food had been so readily available, she hadn't thought about the consequences if she couldn't eat anything to replenish the energy she had expended.

"Can we slow down for minute?" she called to Faen who was just a few feet up ahead. He turned to look at her, and she could see the anxiety sweep across his face. He stopped his horse and jumped off.

"It's just that, I feel…" He caught her just as she passed out and slid off the side of her horse.

"Faedra. Oh no, Faedra!" He shook her gently, she managed to open her eyes just a crack. "Faedra, stay with me," he coaxed then looked up at his sister. "Jocelyn, we don't have too much further to the portal, we will have to fly from here."

Jocelyn got down from her horse, her face was full of concern, too.

"I shouldn't have let her… and for so long," Faen chastised himself.

"Brother, you did not know what it would do to her. Do not blame yourself." Jocelyn attempted to sooth her brother's concerns "She will be alright, we will get her some food."

Faen scooped Faedra up in his arms and lifted them both from the ground. He turned to the horses. "Return to the castle," he commanded, and they turned in the opposite direction and sped off at a gallop. Faen and Jocelyn flew like the wind towards the portal.

“I’m sorry, Faedra,” he whispered as he looked into her lifeless face.

“Todmus,” Jocelyn suddenly cried a few minutes later. “Todmus will have some food.”

“Of Course he will. Sister you are a genius, why didn’t I think of that? Jocelyn, you can fly faster than me. Tell Todmus we need a glass of sugar water and any sweet food he may have.”

She nodded, and flew off ahead of her brother.

“We are almost there, Faedra, hang on for just a little longer.”

When they arrived at the portal Todmus and Jocelyn were waiting for them with a tall glass of sugar water and a plate of sweet pastry. Faen lowered Faedra’s limp body to the ground and sat down next to her, leaning her up against him. He held out his hand and Todmus stepped forwards and passed him the glass.

“Faedra,” he shook her shoulders hard, “wake up, Faedra. You have to wake up for me, do you hear!” He was shouting at her with just a hint of desperation in his voice.

“Faedra, Wake up!” he yelled.

He heaved a sigh of relief when he heard a weak groan.

“Drink this,” he said, as he held the glass to her lips and tipped some of its contents into her mouth. Jocelyn and Todmus stood over them, holding their breath.

Faedra took a few sips, and it felt like the sugar surged through her bloodstream as soon as she swallowed it, like an electrical current running through a piece of equipment forcing it to come alive. It felt as if someone had plugged her in, giving her an energy source, and she could feel her body come to life again. The sips turned to gulps as she regained her strength, and by the time she had finished the glass her eyes were wide open and their sparkle had returned. Within minutes the color returned to her cheeks and the dark circles around her eyes disappeared.

Todmus and Jocelyn let out the breath they had been holding, and Todmus stepped forward to give Faedra a sweet sugary pastry.

She gave the little man an appreciative smile. "Thank you, Mr. Todmus."

Todmus blushed. "Oh please, Miss, just call me Todmus."

A few more moments passed and Faedra could feel her strength was almost back to normal.

"Wow that stuff works really well," she said of the sugar water as she pushed herself up off the ground to stand up after she had finished eating the pastry. "I'm going to have to bottle a load up and keep a supply of it in my car from now on. Let's go and get that book. Thanks again, Todmus," she whispered as she walked past him and followed Faen and Jocelyn into the portal.

He nodded his head and smiled at her fondly. "Any time, Miss, come back and see us again soon."

Then the three of them were gone from Azran and were stepping onto the gravel path that ran behind the church. It was still light. Faedra wasn't quite sure what to expect when she stepped foot in the World of Men again. She only hoped and prayed that Faen was right, and that it was still Sunday, otherwise her father would be sick with worry, and she would have some serious explaining to do. Talking of explaining, she had to come up with an excuse to not be at home that evening. Where she thought the book might be was several hours' drive away. They would be lucky to get there and back before the next morning.

They walked towards her car. The car park was empty now apart from hers. "Are we in glamour?" she asked Faen as they approached the car.

"Yes," he answered.

"Would you two turn into your furry alter egos and un-glamour us then?"

Faen gave her a puzzled look.

"The vicar is over there and I want to ask him something."

"Consider it done," Faen said as he and Jocelyn shimmered and blurred into their dog forms.

The vicar looked a little bemused as he caught sight of Faedra, and he looked around himself. "Good afternoon, Faedra, I didn't see you approaching."

"Hello, Vicar. Beautiful Sunday afternoon isn't it?" she asked covertly.

"It most certainly is my dear, I was just getting ready for evening service."

Faedra inwardly heaved a sigh of relief. It *was* still Sunday. Her secret was safe.

"Have you got yourself another dog?" the vicar asked, looking down at Jocelyn who was sitting to one side of her, and Faen to the other. She had a feeling Jocelyn was going to be spending a lot of time with her from now on and answered accordingly.

"Yes, Vicar I have, she's pretty isn't she?"

"That she is, Faedra, well you have a lovely evening."

He wandered off towards the church, and Faedra headed towards her car with Faen and Jocelyn hot on her heels. She let Jocelyn in the back and Faen in the front passenger side. She knew they would change as soon as she started to drive away. They did.

"How far away is the book do you think?" Faen asked as they drove down the lane past the stables. They went past a field, and a farmer who was standing at the edge of his ruined field of corn scratching his head, momentarily distracted Faedra.

"Um, about five or six hours by car," she answered.

"So what do you intend to tell your father about your pending absence?"

She looked over at him. "I'll think of something." She was an adult now and it's not like it was a school night, she wasn't at school anymore. She wiggled in her seat so she could pry the cell phone out of her back pocket, flipped it open, and dialed.

"Hi, Amy, it's me. Hey, I need you to do a favor for me," she spoke urgently into the phone.

"Sure, Fae, whaddya need?"

"I need you to cover for me tonight."

"Why what are you up to?" Amy asked suspiciously.

"Amy, if I told you, you wouldn't believe me," Faedra replied with honesty.

"You're sneaking off with Frederick aren't you. God he's hot, Fae, I wouldn't blame you."

Faedra almost reprimanded her friend for her dirty mind, and then thought twice about it. Amy would gladly cover for her if she thought she was having fun. Amy lived to have fun. "Er, you got me, Ames. So I'm going to tell my dad that I'm coming round yours tonight for a sleep over. If he should call, which I doubt he would coz I have my phone, but if he does, tell him I'm in the bathroom or something."

"On one condition," Amy demanded.

"What's that?" Faedra asked cautiously.

"You tell me all about it. I want details."

Faedra cringed. More lying, she hated lying. "Of course, Amy, that goes without saying."

"Consider it done then, have fun, Fae and don't do anything I wouldn't do," she laughed, and rang off.

Faedra shook her head and smiled. She loved her friend to death, but hated having to lie to her and her dad.

A few minutes later they were driving down the little dirt road that led to her home. The cottage looked beautiful. She hadn't realized quite how much she had missed it until it came into view. The garden however, was a different story. The flowers were wilting and the leaves still falling. She parked the car and let Faen and Jocelyn, who were now back in their furry forms, out.

"Hi, Dad," she said cheerily as she walked into the living room. Her dad was still fixatedly watching the television. "Don't tell me you've been watching that all day?"

He pulled his gaze away from the screen for a moment. "Oh hello, darling, did you have a good ride?"

"Yes thanks," she said. It wasn't really a lie she had had two good rides since she'd seen him last. It was just that neither of them were on Gypsy.

He looked down and saw Jocelyn sitting beside Faen. "Who's this?"

"She is always hanging around the church and she seems to get on with Faen. The vicar said she must be a stray, so I thought I'd bring her home see if she likes it. You don't mind do you?"

He thought about it for a second. "You're old enough to look after them, Fae, it's fine with me."

"Thanks, Dad," she wandered over to give him a kiss on the cheek. "You're the best."

"You only say that because I let you have your own way most of the time," he said with a smirk.

Faedra ruffled his hair. "Speaking of letting me have my own way. I've been invited to a sleep over at Amy's tonight, you don't have a problem with that do you?"

"No, of course not, darling, you go and have fun."

"So has anything changed with the situation?" she asked, looking at the TV with him. "Have they come up with any ideas yet?"

"Nope, not a thing. All the scientists are completely baffled."

"Hmm," Faedra responded, "well I'll leave you to it. I'm going to get ready for tonight." She walked towards the kitchen. Once there she rummaged in some cupboards for the supplies she would need.

"Okay, I need bottles of water and a bag of sugar," she talked to herself while grabbing those things, then proceeded to make a load of sandwiches. It was going to be a long night, and all three of them needed to eat.

She ran up to her bedroom and grabbed her sports bag from the closet. Dumped its contents onto the floor, and ran back down the stairs again. The bag was the perfect size for their supplies.

"One more thing," she said to Faen and Jocelyn, who were sitting patiently on the kitchen floor watching her industriously assemble the necessities they would need. She walked out of the kitchen and into her father's office. She scanned the shelves, not there. She opened and closed drawers. "Oh come on, I know there's one in here somewhere." She looked in a couple more drawers. "Yes," she said as she pulled out a road map of England.

"Okay, I think we're ready," she announced as she walked back into the kitchen, shoved the map into her bag and threw the bag over her shoulder. All three wandered back through the dining room and into the living room.

"I'm off now, Dad," she announced, and planted another kiss on his cheek. "Love you."

"Love you, too, darling, have fun."

"I will," she lied, and the three cohorts hurried out the door and started loading up the car.

They drove for hours and it broke Faedra's heart to see the dying countryside flashing by them. England was usually so green, and it made her more determined than ever to get the book back, but up until that point she hadn't given a thought as to how they would actually go about that particular task. Bearing in mind that she had even deciphered Kernnunos' vision correctly in the first place. She prayed that she wasn't taking them all on a wild goose chase. The book had to be there it just had to be.

"Faen, have you given any thought to how we are going to retrieve the book from whoever has it? I mean they must be pretty powerful to have been able to get it in the first place."

She didn't like the look he gave her it was not his usual look of confidence. It smacked of 'I haven't thought that far ahead, we'll just make it up as we go along and hope for the best'.

"I am afraid that until we know what or who we are dealing with I will not know what course of action to take," he replied.

"In other words, you don't have a plan."

"No," he agreed. Well at least he was being honest.

Faedra wished that where they were headed wasn't so far away. Her mind had a tendency to wander if she drove for any length of time, and right now it had far too much time on its hands, and was working overtime. Worst case scenarios were playing themselves out in her head left, right and center, and none of them had a happy ending for her, or her friends. She hated being a worrywart sometimes.

She sincerely hoped that she wouldn't have to come face to face with any more Redcaps, but considering her history with them so far, she thought it was a bit too much to hope for. At least she knew her powers could knock them out cold. She leaned over, grabbed a bottle, and drank some more sugar water at the thought.

Jocelyn and Faen were eerily silent. She could sense that Faen was trying to figure out some sort of plan, but as yet hadn't come up with anything. As for Jocelyn, Faedra now felt horrible about getting her involved in this. She was such a sweet girl, she couldn't bear it if she got hurt.

"Jocelyn, maybe you should stay in the car when we get there," Faedra said voicing her concern.

"Are you kidding me?" Jocelyn replied. "I have been dying for some action for eons now, there is no way I am missing this."

"Oh," Faedra said with surprise. "Well, just thought I would give you the option."

"Faedra, I am not silent because I am worried. I am silent because I am preparing myself," Jocelyn explained after she realized why Faedra was giving her an out.

"Some little sister you've got there," she chuckled to Faen.

"Yes, she does have her moments," he agreed with a proud smile.

The sun was starting to set as Faedra noticed one of the landmarks that Kernunnos had mentioned.

"Look," she pointed towards a large mound. "Silbury Hill, 'a hill that is perfectly round'. It is a man made hill, built about 4600 years ago, and has a perfectly round base. We are getting close."

They drove a little further and she pointed to something up on a hillside. Faen and Jocelyn peered out of the windows, and followed where she was pointing. " 'Giant white horses'. There are eight white chalk horses carved into the hillsides around this area," she explained.

A little further and the next landmark came into view. " 'A spire so high it touches the sky'. Salisbury Cathedral, it has one of the tallest spires in Europe. And just down here a little way we should see it."

A little while later she saw it loom eerily into view. It was almost dark now, and the full moon was rising behind it. The magical aura this place exuded was not lost on her.

"And there it is, Stonehenge, 'a circle of stone, surrounded by A's'. The A303 and the A344 to be precise," she pointed to the road sign up ahead. "The two roads that run either side of it."

"Well done, Faedra," Jocelyn exclaimed. "However did you figure it out?"

"I've been here before. Mum brought me when I was little. I remember her telling me how important this place was," she sighed at the memory.

Stonehenge rose up majestically before them as they drove closer and closer to it. Faedra turned off the road into the car park that was purposely built for tourists. It was empty this late at night. Stonehenge was “Closed”. She laughed at the irony of it. How could a mythical ancient monument, thousands of years old, standing in the middle of a field be “Closed”.

She parked the car and they made their way across the road. Her heart was pounding now. She had no idea what to expect when they actually got to the circle.

“Oh no,” she exclaimed as they made it across the road. “It’s been fenced off, it wasn’t fenced off when I came here before.”

A tall chain link fence now encircled the ancient monolithic stones, allowing only those who would pay, to see it up close.

“How do we get in now?”

Faen and Jocelyn looked at her incredulously.

“What?” she asked, narrowing her eyes at them.

They each linked an arm around one of hers, lifted themselves and her off the ground, and glided effortlessly over the fence.

“Oh,” she stated as her cheeks burned with embarrassment.

CHAPTER FIFTEEN

They moved towards the standing stones making as little noise as possible. Faedra could feel her ring heating up on her finger and looked down at it. The symbols were glowing fiercely in the darkness. Her heart was in her mouth, but they could not yet see anyone or anything. The monoliths grew taller and taller as they approached. Faedra couldn't help but think how impressive the stones were when they were towering above her.

Upon reaching the outer circle they stopped. Faen was scanning all around them, both him and Jocelyn on high alert. He extricated his sword from its sheath and held it in both hands out in front of him. Jocelyn mumbled something that Faedra couldn't understand, and an exquisitely engraved sword appeared in her hands from nowhere. She took the same stance as her brother. Faedra's eyes widened with surprise at the way Jocelyn looked so at ease holding her sword.

They moved with caution between the stones. Faedra was flanked either side by Faen and Jocelyn. They saw nothing, heard nothing, but Faedra knew something was there. Her ring was screaming at her now, and telling her just that. They made it to the center of the circle and looked around them. The moon was high in the sky and bathing the entire area in an unearthly silver glow, causing the monoliths to cast large dark shadows all around them.

"I wondered how long it would take you," a female voice, as smooth as silk echoed out of the darkness.

All three turned in the direction of the voice and scanned thc shadows. Faedra's heart was beating so hard she thought it would punch itself right out of her chest. They could still see no one. A second later a scraping noise, like someone running nails along a chalkboard, resonated high in front of them, and they looked up. A woman was walking across one of the lintel stones, dragging a sword on the stone behind her that was sending sparks flying spectacularly into the air. She was also holding a book, *The* book.

The woman was tall and slender. Under the silvery light it looked like her hair was raven black and fell half way down her back in a tumble of luscious sleek waves. Her skin was pale and held the same luminescent quality that Faen's and Jocelyn's did. She wore a long opulent blue dress of pure silk that shimmered in the moonlight, and her spectacular wings of snow white were outstretched to either side of her. She was beautiful, regally beautiful.

"Your Highness?" Faen questioned with a puzzled expression.

"Very observant, Guardian." her voice remained smooth as silk, but her expression wrinkled into a sneer.

An awkward silence hovered around them as they all, one by one, digested the scene unfolding before their eyes.

"Vivianna?" Faen questioned in disbelief. "You took the book? You tortured Elvelynn? But she was your friend."

Vivianna laughed, a cold heartless laugh. "I do not get my hands dirty on such mundane tasks, Guardian," she sneered, "I have my… little helpers to do that for me."

Movement among the stones below Vivianna distracted Faedra, and a dozen pairs of glowing yellow eyes appeared in the shadows. She sucked in a breath, and Faen and Jocelyn moved in closer to her until they were almost touching.

"But why?" Faen continued his line of questioning. "Why would you want to destroy our world and this one?"

"I have my reasons," she replied, her voice still silken, but she shot an icy glare towards Faedra.

Faedra looked up into the dark night sky, for what she didn't know. Maybe some kind of sign that they would get through this, some kind of inspiration. Although, from where she was standing the odds looked pretty well stacked against them. Her attention was caught by a streak of luminescent light that wavered ethereally across the sky above her. It was mesmerizing in its beauty, and shimmered with all the colors of the rainbow. Then there was another and another until it looked like she was watching the Aurora Borealis. She nudged Faen.

"What is it is, Faedra?" he asked. His eyes still fixated on Vivianna.

"Look," she said, still looking at the sky above her.

He turned his gaze to her and followed her line of sight. A blank expression superceded the one of concern that was previously there.

"What it is?" she whispered when she noticed that his look was one of recognition. He had seen this before.

He said nothing.

"Faen?" she urged.

"Valkyries," he responded stoically.

More movement on the opposite side of the circle to where the Redcaps were hiding in the shadows made them turn and look. Faedra's jaw dropped as she watched seven enormous winged horses maneuver with stealth through the stones and came to a stop just beyond the shadows. Each horse was black as midnight with shining, flame red eyes that glowed ominously in the darkness. They were snorting fiercely as they furled their outstretched wings to nestle them along their flanks.

Sitting astride each horse was a beautiful maiden. Each of them wearing a silken white dress but their torsos were protected by armor, and they each wore a helmet and were carrying a spear in an outstretched arm. Faedra could see now where the lights in the sky were coming from. Each plate of armor sparkled under the moonlight like the facets of a diamond caught under the halogen lights in a jewelry store.

"Valkyrics?" Faedra choked. "What are Valkyries doing here?"

"I do not know," Faen responded, regarding them with interest and not taking his eyes from them.

"But don't Valkyries come to watch over a battle?"

"Yes."

"And then take the slain back to Valhalla to become warriors?"

Faen took his eyes off the Valkyries for a second and regarded Faedra with the same interest. "You have done your homework," he said with a raise of his eyebrow.

She shrugged. "What can I say, mythology fascinates me, and it's amazing what you can find on the Internet," she gave him a weak smile, which he returned before reverting his gaze back to the armored maidens.

"Oh God," Faedra whispered under her breath after being given a moment to think about it. Her body started to tremble, it was involuntary on her part, but nevertheless, seemed to be out of her control. She wasn't ready to die and fight for Odin for all eternity.

Faen took hold of her hand and gave it a squeeze in an attempt to calm her. He could sense her getting frayed around the edges and they all needed to focus if they were going to make it through this.

"We do not know why they are here, Faedra, do not trouble yourself just yet. Asgard and Valhalla are probably just as much affected as Azran and The World of Men, if Vivianna is trying to destroy all realms she certainly has it within her grasp to do so. The book controls nature in *every* realm not just ours."

The winged horses stepped forward until they were lined up in front of them. The center horse then broke ranks and moved closer to the three that were huddled back to back in a protective triangle in the center of the circle. Restless murmuring came from where the Redcaps were lurking in the shadows, but they did not move forward themselves.

Vivianna stood on the lintel above them, watching with amusement as the scene played out below her. A vindictive smile curved her lips. This was more than she could have hoped for, that the Valkyries would take them to fight for eternity after she had slaughtered them. They would never have the chance to rest in peace after all, and this thought made her intensely happy.

The solo winged horse came to a stop just feet away from Faen, and Faedra assumed it must be carrying the leader of the group. She had not been able to take her eyes from the maiden who exuded grace and valor, but there was an underlying presence that was unmistakable. These maidens were not here to take sides, they were here to take the losers. Faedra's heart sank once more. For a second she had allowed herself a glimmer of hope that they would help because their world may be suffering, too, but without words it was still as clear as crystal that the Valkyries would not be breaking any rules that night.

The maiden and Faen exchanged pointed glances at each other in silence for a moment.

"Freja," Faen broke the silence first.

Freja inclined her head in acknowledgement. "Guardian," she responded, and Faen did the same. They fell silent again but neither one broke eye contact with the other.

"I think that we have had quite enough of the pleasantries," Vivianna's silken voice cut through the silence like a knife.

The Valkyries looked up at her, and Freja nodded her head in agreement. She looked to the maidens on one side of her and then the other, and their horses all simultaneously backed up until they were lined against the inner wall of the circle.

"They're not going to help us are they?" Faedra whispered to Faen.

"They cannot be seen to be aiding us, no," he replied.

That at least gave Faedra a glimmer of hope. He hadn't just said 'no, end of story'.

As soon as the Valkyries had retreated Vivianna flew down and landed on the altar stone towards the center of the circle.

"Let us have some fun, shall we?" she said as she lay the Book of Anohs down on the alter stone. "I will give you the chance to win back the book, Custodian," she taunted, then mumbled something under her breath and another sword appeared in her other hand. She swiveled them around her body in a spectacular display of sword skills. Even Faedra had to admit she looked impressive, which certainly didn't help with the knots that were tying themselves in her stomach.

"Vivianna," Faen reprimanded, "Faedra does not know the way of the sword. You dishonor our race by what you ask."

"Do you think I care of honor or dishonor after I found out about *her!*" Vivianna spat her words that were full of anger and contempt. She threw one of the swords hilt first for Faedra to catch.

To Faedra's surprise she caught the sword gracefully, and the feeling of holding it in her hands was an oddly familiar one. She couldn't understand why, she had never held a sword before this moment.

She looked up at Vivianna. "I don't even know you, what could I have possibly done to offend you?" she asked, trying in vain to hide the quiver in her voice.

Vivianna looked at her intently, carefully measuring Faedra's expression. "You do not know do you?" Vivianna narrowed her eyes, but her voice was smooth as silk again.

"Know what?" Faedra questioned.

"Oh, this makes things even better," Vivianna laughed, a cold hard cackle that made Faedra shudder. "After I kill you and retrieve the amulet, I will send you to your grave forever ignorant of who you are."

"What is she talking about, Faen?" Faedra whispered.

"I do not know."

"Silence!" Vivianna bellowed as she swooped down from the altar and was standing a few feet in front of Faedra. "Kill them, leave the *samtero kruwos* for me," she commanded in the direction of the Redcaps.

Faedra saw Jocelyn and Faen exchange surprised glances at the foreign sounding words Vivianna had just spoken in reference to herself. But a second later the Redcaps had surrounded them and they were busy defending themselves.

"Fight!" Vivianna instructed Faedra, and slammed hard with her sword. It clashed forcefully with Faedra's, knocking her off balance and sending her crashing to the ground. Vivianna hovered above her, horizontal to the ground, holding her sword point to Faedra's throat. "Don't bore me, Custodian, get up," she demanded as she landed back on the ground and stepped back, allowing Faedra to get to her feet.

Faedra picked up the sword, her heart pounding. She didn't know how to fight with a sword. She looked over to where Faen and Jocelyn were expertly wielding theirs. She could hear their swords clashing with the Redcap's axe-like weapons, and so far could see two of the evil beings dead on the ground. She gulped, she wouldn't last five seconds if she were expected to know how to use a sword to that proficiency.

Vivianna came at her once more with a force that Faedra could see was going to knock her off her feet again. She braced herself, and held her sword out in front of her tightly in both hands, trying hard not to close her eyes as Vivianna's made contact with hers and sent sparks flying. The swords connected with such intensity Faedra could feel the vibration fly up her arms and into her head. Vivianna came at her low the next time, and Faedra angled her sword to meet the blow and defend her legs.

The Redcaps were fast, they were coming at Faen and Jocelyn from all angles. Jocelyn hovered above the ground to dodge the axe that was being wielded towards her but another Redcap grabbed her neck with his invisible hold and threw her violently against one of the stones. She lay stunned for a few seconds, but regained her senses just in time to move to the side, narrowly missing the spear part of the weapon as it came at her head but made contact with the stone instead. She got up and spun round to the back of the stone, and leaned against it for a few seconds to catch her breath before moving round to enter the battle again.

Faen's sword was flying in all directions, clashing fiercely with his enemies' weapons. Four Redcaps surrounded him, and before they had had a chance to respond he had raised himself from the ground and flew over one of them, stabbing it without mercy in the back. It fell to the ground with a thud. Another then grabbed him with the same invisible force and held him up above the ground. Faen struggled in mid air, but the stranglehold the Redcap had on him was so strong it forced Faen to drop his sword, which landed point down and was standing up in the earth below him. Jocelyn saw what was happening, and with lightening speed, crossed to the Redcap holding her brother and slashed it through the chest. It slumped to the ground, and Faen caught himself just before he hit the ground and was able to land softly. He grabbed his sword and wielded it round as he spun towards yet another Redcap, taking it out with a fatal blow to the head.

With a move that Faedra didn't even know her body knew existed, she spun round wielding her sword around her head, and brought it crashing to meet Vivianna's. They hit so hard that sparks flew on contact.

Vivianna had a satisfied glint to her eye. "That is more like it, Custodian, this will be so much more fun than when I killed your mother. I didn't have any time to play with her, and I find poison such a boring way to kill."

Faedra stepped back, reeling from what she had just heard, and Vivianna caught her off guard again with a swing to her upper body, slicing through her shirt and into her arm.

"Ouch!" Faedra screamed. She looked down at her arm just as she caught sight of Vivianna's blade coming at her again. She somehow ducked under it and was now standing behind her. She could feel the blood pouring down her arm, but now that there was revenge flowing through it, it didn't seem to hurt as much. Vivianna spun round so she was facing her opponent, ready to wield another blow at Faedra. Pure fury flowed through Faedra and she charged at Vivianna, wielding her sword around her head. It clashed so hard with her opponent's that it was nearly knocked out of her hands.

"Your sword skills are very rudimentary," Vivianna said with an undeniable pleasure.

"You don't say," Faedra retorted sarcastically, and slammed her sword hard into Vivianna's, forcing the fairy to step back, "well considering this is the first time I've ever held one, I would hazard a guess that I'm going to be good enough to kick your fairy butt all the way back to Azran."

Vivianna laughed her cold humorless laugh.

"Why did you kill my mother?" Faedra demanded between the wielding of swords and the clashing of blades. Their swords locked at the hand guard so their faces were mere inches from one another.

"She stumbled upon my Redcaps plotting the execution of my plan and was about to enter Azran to tell my father, I could not allow that to happen. I was so close to taking the amulet then, but Faen showed up," she scowled, "so I have spent the past eleven of your years biding my time until you became of age." Her silken voice did not fool Faedra, she knew the owner of it was deadly. Vivianna used the hand guard of her sword and pushed hard on Faedra's, forcing Faedra to stumble backwards.

"But why would you turn on your father and your own people, not to mention my people? Everyone is suffering

Vivianna," Faedra cried as she tried desperately to regain her balance and stay upright.

Vivianna eyed Faedra with vicious intent, holding her sword out in front of her ready for another attack.

"Revenge, Custodian, pure and simple," she came at Faedra faster and more determined than ever. "Let us see what havoc I can wreak when I have control over weather, too."

Faedra was desperate to know what Vivianna wanted revenge for, but Vivianna's determination caught Faedra off guard again and she went to make several defensive steps back, but was blocked by something hard in the small of her back. She looked round to see it was the alter stone. Vivianna was on her almost immediately, but Faedra had not managed to adjust her grip on her sword, and with the next blow it was sent flying from her hands. Vivianna raised her sword with malevolence and was about to wield a fatal blow, but Faedra was not ready to die just yet. She had questions that needed answering, and if that fact alone was giving her the determination needed to survive, that was just fine with her.

She was lying half on, half off the altar stone, and with a movement of pure adrenaline she rolled her body over and Vivianna's sword missed her by mere millimeters, clashing with such a force on the stone beside her she could feel it vibrate. She slid off the other end of the stone and moved quickly around it, putting it between her and Vivianna, looking around her for her sword as she did. She couldn't see it. *Oh God, where did it go?*

She looked up just in time to see Vivianna fly up on top of the stone and was now standing above her with her sword poised to swipe at Faedra's head. It was a knee jerk reaction; Faedra held her hands up and closed her eyes, as two balls of blue light thrust themselves forcefully from her palms, knocking both her and Vivianna off their feet with the intensity, but not for long enough. Faedra hadn't had the time to focus on her energy to make it powerful enough to do much damage.

Vivianna was on her feet again in seconds and was flying towards Faedra who scrabbled backwards on the ground, using her legs and feet to push her backwards with all her might. She scanned the ground around her and could see her sword a few feet out of her reach. Her heart sank she knew she would not be able to reach it in time.

Her eyes widened as she saw the sword turn and skim along the ground hilt first until it reached her hand. She looked up just in time to see the Valkyrie nearest to her return her spear to her side and look away with an innocent expression on her face. Grabbing her sword she held it above her head defensively just as Vivianna's came crashing down with another blow to try and take her head off.

Faedra's phone rang. She could tell it was her father, she had a specific ring tone for him.

"Oh crap," she groaned. *Great timing Dad*, she thought as she defended against an onslaught of blows from Vivianna. If she didn't answer it he would just call Amy, and she really didn't want her friend to have to lie for her if at all possible. She shot another energy ball at Vivianna, knocking her backwards, and grabbed the phone from her pocket.

"Hi, Dad," she grunted breathlessly, "you kind of caught me at a bad time, can I call you back?"

"Sure, darling, what on earth is all that commotion?"

"Err, we're playing *Dungeons and Dragons* on Amy's video game – Urgh," she groaned as she shot another energy ball and sent Vivianna reeling backwards again.

"You sound pretty out of breath, hun."

"Well it's one of those remotes you have to use like the real thing. At the moment I'm having an – argh – swordfight with an – urgh – evil fairy princess, it's really interactive."

"Oh, okay, darling, well have fun, I hope you win."

"Me too, Dad, me too," she rang off and moved her head to one side just in time to dodge another blow that came crashing to the ground. She looked at her phone that she was still clutching and threw it away as she grabbed for her sword .

She held it with one hand and threw another energy ball with the other, forcing Vivianna back just long enough for Faedra to get to her feet. Then she saw the book, it was still sitting on the end of the altar stone where Vivianna had laid it before they had started their fight. She had to think of a way to get her hands on it, but right now she was being well and truly out-sworded by her opponent, and it was all she could do to keep herself from getting killed.

Use the amulet, Faedra.

"Mum?" Faedra called out, looking all around her. Vivianna stopped for just a second and gave her a questioning glance, then continued with her onslaught.

The amulet, Faedra, use the amulet.

She couldn't quite believe she was having a *Star Wars* moment with her mother, but went with it. "How do I use the amulet, Mum?" she cried out into the darkness as she sent another energy ball into Vivianna's chest to distract her for another few seconds.

Think, Faedra, the book is near. Use your power to use the amulet

"That's all I need right now, riddles," she mumbled under her breath. How on earth could she get hold of the book when she was fighting for her life. Vivianna was not giving her any respite, where did this woman get her energy. She looked around her in the split seconds she had between parries, and shooting energy balls. The red eyes of the winged horses shone in the darkness, the Valkyries sitting motionless, were watching intently, but with no movement to imply that they would help again.

Faen and Jocelyn were still wielding their swords valiantly. There were fewer Redcaps now, which gave her an idea. It was a long shot but if Jocelyn could hold off the Redcaps and Faen could distract Vivianna, maybe it would give her enough time to figure out how to use the book and the amulet.

"Faen!" she cried out across the circle. Her sword clashed with Vivianna's sending more sparks flying.

"Yes!" he shouted back.

Vivianna was upon her again. Faedra swung her sword just in time to meet with her opponent's and averted the loss of a limb.

"Do you think Jocelyn can handle those Redcaps by herself for a minute?" Crash, she dodged another blow that struck the altar stone, sending more sparks flying.

There was silence for a moment, except for the clashing of metal on metal.

"I think so," Jocelyn shouted back.

"Faen, distract this evil fairy for a moment would you?" Faedra asked and shot an icy glare at Vivianna who just smiled at her vindictively as she came at the Custodian again with her sword.

"It would be my pleasure," he spoke with deep satisfaction as he flew over and descended upon Vivianna with a clash of his sword, giving her no choice than to give up her onslaught on Faedra.

Vivianna screamed something incoherent at Faedra, who could see the fury in her eyes.

Faedra dropped her sword, dodged past the two of them who were fighting with a vengeance and grabbed the Book of Anohs from the altar. The stone in the amulet blazed to life as she ran with the book into the shadow of a monolithic stone.

"How do I do this? Oh God, what do I do?" she mumbled as she looked over to her two friends who were fighting for their lives. "Well whatever you do, Faedra," she told herself, "do it quickly." She opened the book, but found that of no help, it was written in a language she couldn't understand. Then she had an idea, what if she imagined the weather she wanted, would that work? Could it be that easy? She took hold of the amulet, closed her eyes, and concentrated. A moment passed and she could feel cold splashes on her face, she opened her eyes and looked up. Dark clouds had appeared from nowhere and it was suddenly raining - hard. Within seconds she was drenched through to the skin.

"Ha," she cried, "it worked."

"Not… helping…!" Faen grunted over his shoulder between parries with Vivianna.

Faedra closed her eyes again and the rain stopped as abruptly as it had started. "Sorry," she called out to her now soggy cohorts who she could see slipping on the wet ground. "That was stupid, Faedra," she cursed at herself.

She glanced over to see how Jocelyn was doing and was horror struck as she watched a Redcap sneak up and spear her from behind. Jocelyn gasped and slumped to the ground.

"NO!" Faedra yelled as anger surged through her more blindingly than she'd ever felt it before. Thunder roiled ominously in the air around her, a low growl to begin with that turned rapidly into a noise so vicious the sky sounded like it was being ripped apart.

She could feel her body surging with an energy so powerful it was overwhelming, and held her hands up to the sky, asking for more, accepting every tiny particle the atmosphere could provide her. At that moment a bolt of lightening struck her in the heart, but instead of it killing her she absorbed it, molded it, her whole body crackled loudly. Then she realized it was her that was making the noise, not the thunder.

She opened her eyes, which were now glowing with the bright blue-white radiance of the lightening she had absorbed, and threw her hands out in the direction of the Redcaps, unleashing every particle of electrical energy she had molded inside of her. Six bolts of lightening flew from her palms hitting each Redcap directly in the chest and killing them on contact. They slumped to the ground also. Faedra fell back against the stone and attempted to steady herself, she could feel her legs weaken beneath her.

Vivianna was momentarily distracted by Faedra's show of power, enough that Faen had been able to knock the sword from her hand and was now holding his to her throat. He kicked Vivianna's sword out of reach.

With the last fragment of will that Faedra had left, she stumbled over to where Jocelyn lay unmoving on the wet ground. She sat down beside her and lifted Jocelyn's head, cradling it in her arms.

"Jocelyn, oh no. Please God, not Jocelyn." Big fat tears rolled down Faedra's cheeks as she carefully moved a clump of wet hair that was splayed across her friend's lifeless face. She looked over to Faen in desperation, tears flowing freely down her face. He was still standing motionless, holding his sword to Vivianna's throat.

"Oh, Faen," she cried, "I think she's dead."

Faen's eyes blazed with an anger Faedra had never seen before. He swung his sword high above his head and was just about to wield it with a fatal blow to Vivianna's neck when Jocelyn coughed. He stopped mid swing and looked over to where Faedra and Jocelyn were on the ground.

Jocelyn breathed in, an urgent gasp as if coming up for air after being submerged under water. She opened her eyes slowly and smiled up at Faedra.

"You're alive?" Faedra half laughed, half cried, she was so overjoyed.

"They must have missed my heart," Jocelyn whispered, her voice sounding gravelly.

"She's alive, Faen," Faedra called.

Vivianna took advantage of the distraction and flew over Faen's head to stand behind him on the alter stone. Faen whirled round but just as he did, she spat some more words that Faedra did not recognize, and something appeared in her hand. At first glance it looked like a small gnarly tree branch, but it glittered with sparkling red stones. Vivianna glared at Faen and then over at Faedra, she muttered something else and slammed the staff hard on the stone.

The red stones emitted what looked like whirling red laser lights that within seconds had encircled Vivianna.

She gave Faen a malevolent smile "Until we meet again, Guardian," she said smoothly with an incline of her head.

"No," Faen cried, and lunged out with his sword, but she was gone, and it came crashing to the stone. He shouted something Faedra didn't understand and from his tone of voice, wasn't sure she wanted to either. He sheathed his sword angrily and strode over to where the girls were sitting on the ground. His expression altered in an instant as soon as he reached them, replacing the one of anger with one of compassion.

"Jocelyn," he cupped her face, his eyes full of concern. "My dear sister, are you alright?"

She smiled at him. "I am fine, Brother, it missed my heart."

Faen hung his head and heaved a sigh of relief. They looked at the bodies that were strewn all around them.

"Where did Vivianna go?" Faedra asked. "And what was that thing she had?"

"It was the Ruby Staff," he replied. "It has the power to transport you in an instant to anywhere in any realm. I have only ever heard of it, I have never seen it before. It holds dark magic, I do not know how she came by it, I was told it had been destroyed."

They had been so focused on Jocelyn they hadn't noticed that the Valkyries had advanced, and were now forming a semi circle around them. Freja moved forward from the line again.

"Well done," she said to all three, her features devoid of emotion. "Redcaps make excellent warriors."

All of the maidens held out their spears, and lowered them so they were pointing at the bodies on the floor, and Faedra watched as the Redcaps shimmered and disappeared.

"Our job here is done, Guardian," Freja continued, "as is yours."

The horses all backed up in one fluid movement and then turned. They walked through the stones of the circle and disappeared.

Faen scooped his injured sister up off the cold, wet ground. Faedra pushed herself up, which took more effort than she could have imagined, and stumbled over to the book. She leaned over and scooped it up, wrapping her arms around it and held it tight to her chest.

"We need to get this back to Azran," she croaked.

"Jocelyn, there must be a portal nearby, can you sense one?" Faen asked.

Jocelyn closed her eyes for a moment and concentrated.

"Yes, Brother there is one at the cathedral we passed, but I do not know where in Azran it will take us," she replied.

"We will have to take our chances," he said as he looked at Faedra, and could see her complexion graying and her legs weaken. Jocelyn noticed, too.

"Brother, take Faedra back to the car, I will wait here until you come back."

Faen looked with concern from his injured sister to his weakening charge.

"Go. I will be fine," Jocelyn reassured him.

The Guardian laid his sister with care on the altar stone and turned to Faedra.

"Come, young lady, we need to get you some sugar water," he scooped Faedra up just as her legs gave way. She smiled at him weakly, she had no energy left to do anything else.

He turned back to his sister. "I will be back in a moment."

CHAPTER SIXTEEN

After Faedra had replenished her energy levels by drinking nearly every bottle of sugar water she had prepared, she drove them to Salisbury Cathedral. It was an impressive building, the spire towered several hundred feet above them. She had read somewhere once that the weather vane on the top of the spire was the size of a donkey.

"This way," Jocelyn pointed, and headed off in the direction of where she could sense the portal.

Jocelyn's body had healed itself in the time it took for them to reach the cathedral, much to her brother and her friend's relief.

Faedra was still holding on tight to the book, and Faen was scanning the area all around them as they followed the younger fairy to the portal. There was no telling where Vivianna could be. It wouldn't surprise the Guardian if she turned up and tried to take the book away, and he wouldn't feel comfortable until it was safely back in the castle and under some stronger magical bonds than last time.

Jocelyn came to a sudden stop, and made a sharp turn. "Over there," she said. She reminded Faedra of a Bloodhound sniffing out a scent. "Here it is," she stated as she came to a sudden stop on the path. Jocelyn recited an incantation, and told Faedra and Faen when the portal was open.

"Get ready with your sword, Jocelyn. We do not know what awaits us on the other side," Faen instructed cautiously.

Jocelyn conjured her sword, and Faen drew his from its sheath. He looked down at Faedra and gave her a wry smile. "As for you my little *Kenget,* I believe you can hold your own. Energy balls at the ready?"

She smiled back at him, her eyes twinkling from the reflection of the ball of blue light that was now bobbing above her free hand.

"What does *Kenget* mean?"

He laughed. "It means Warrior."

Faedra bopped him on the arm with her elbow. "I hardly think so," she blushed. "She out-sworded me every step of the way."

"Faedra, do not underestimate yourself. You had never held a sword before today and survived a fight against one of the best in our realm - Vivianna has been training since she was a child – and you are still alive to tell the tale. To be honest with you, I do not know how you did it," he looked at her with pride. "I believe you will be a formidable Custodian," his smile slipped and his eyes saddened. "I think perhaps, you will not need me anymore."

Panic flashed across Faedra's face. "You're not going to leave me are you?" Her energy ball fizzled out with her question.

He considered her panic-stricken face for a moment and a warm smile curved his lips. "No, Faedra, I will not leave you, unless you wish it. Shall we?" He motioned in the direction of the portal.

Faedra's body relaxed and she smiled back at him, the ball of light reappearing in her palm.

The three of them stepped into the portal on full alert. A second later they were standing in a cobbled street in the City of Azran. People meandered past them, going about their business. Faedra closed her hand, Faen sheathed his sword, and Jocelyn's disappeared.

"Look!" Faedra shouted as she pointed to a window box hanging on a wall nearby. "The flowers, they are growing again." They all wandered over to the window box. Bright green shoots were starting to poke their way through the soil. "It worked, the plants are growing. When I took the book from Vivianna it must have broken whatever hold she had over it. We did it!" She shoved the book at Jocelyn and wrapped her arms around Faen's neck to give him a hug. He picked her up and swung her around, a laugh escaped him as he got caught up in her excitement.

Her outburst had caught the attention of some passers-by, and suddenly gasps of shock and surprise were resonating all around them as people stopped to see. Faen eased Faedra to the ground and they turned to scan the crowd that was now increasing in number by the second with people looking intently at the book.

"They found it!" A man shouted from the crowd. There was silence for a few seconds, then the crowd erupted and surged forward. At first Faedra thought they were in serious trouble, but as soon as she was scooped up and planted on a burly looking fairy's shoulder, and watched as the same thing happened to Jocelyn and Faen, she realized that these people were pleased to see them.

Cheers rung out down the cobbled streets and little children skipped their way in front of them. They were carried through the city until they arrived at the courtyard in front of the castle, where they were lowered carefully to the ground. The people who had been carrying them bowed and stepped back.

"Thank you," they said.

"You're welcome," Faedra responded. She didn't think it sounded quite appropriate under the circumstances, but it was an automatic response that was commonplace in conversation in her world, and was more habit than thought.

The crowd stood in silence as the three of them walked towards the enormous entrance to the castle. The plants in the courtyard were budding again, and fresh new shoots of life were replacing the brown wilted flowers.

The doors opened without Faen rapping on them this time. They walked through and headed towards the Great Hall. As they entered the Great Hall the volume was deafening. It was still full of people, and their cheers upon seeing the three almost raised the rafters. The king stood waiting for them at the end of the room with a warm smile on his face.

Faedra followed etiquette as best she could before handing him the Book of Anohs. He bowed his head to Faedra as he took it, and the room went silent.

"Our realms owe you all a debt of gratitude," he spoke clearly and proudly so that everyone in the hall could hear. "But for now, I hope you will accept a ball in your honor, to be held this evening."

Whispers resonated around the Great Hall, then the king addressed the crowd.

"Tonight I hold a ball, a celebration of life," he stated in his commanding voice. "Everyone is invited."

The volume increased to deafening again, but the king made a gesture with his hands and the crowd fell silent once more.

"Your Majesty," Faen spoke with caution. "There is something more."

The king nodded, and gestured for them to retire to the library room. Once there he sat behind his desk and rested his elbows on the rich mahogany, touching his fingers together.

"Your Majesty, it is about Vivianna," Faen continued.

The king took a deep breath. "She did this, didn't she?" he asked with a heavy heart. Faedra and Jocelyn looked at each other, eyes wide.

"Yes, Sire, how did you know?"

"I had my suspicions, but I tried to deny them. She is my daughter after all," he hung his head. "Where is she now?"

"We do not know, Sire, she had the Ruby Staff," Faen answered.

The king's head shot up and he narrowed his eyes. "Where would she have gotten the Ruby Staff, I thought it had been destroyed?"

"I cannot answer that, Sire," Faen bowed his head.

"Well there is nothing we can do about it at this moment," he looked at all three intently. "You have done well. Our realms will be eternally grateful to you all. Unfortunately, Faedra, your realm will never know how you saved them, I am afraid most of your kind do not have minds open enough to absorb or believe what happened, so it is best that they never know. Well, you had better go and prepare for the ball," he clapped his hands, and the two fairies that had helped them the day before appeared again.

Faen and Jocelyn turned to follow the fairies who were heading for the door.

"Hold on a moment," Faedra piped up. She had some questions, and thought she deserved some answers. After all, his daughter had just got through trying to make mincemeat out of her. She had some for Faen, too, he was not getting off lightly either. She wanted to know what Vivianna had called her that made Jocelyn and Faen exchange such surprised glances.

Faen could sense the king needed time to absorb the news about Vivianna, and now would not be the right time to be asking him questions. He took hold of Faedra's hand and started to pull her with him. When she gave him a questioning look, he subtly shook his head.

"But…" she replaced the questioning look with one of annoyance.

"Not now, Faedra," he whispered, and looked with concern at the king.

Faedra looked at the king, too. He was holding his head in his hands and was in obvious distress. She conceded that maybe now wasn't the right time to start firing questions at him. It could wait until tomorrow, but she would get some answers, of that she was determined.

"I've got some for you, too," she warned Faen as they followed the fairies through the castle.

"I am sure you do," he replied stoically, but at that point he wasn't quite sure how he was going to answer the one he knew without a doubt she would ask. He was, therefore, relieved when she didn't say anything else, and they walked in silence for the rest of the way to their rooms.

Faedra decided her questions could wait until the next day. She had to admit she was getting excited about being the guest of honor at a fae ball.

The fairies escorted them up to the same rooms they had been given before, and they left them after announcing that if they needed anything to let them know.

"Faen," Faedra whispered with a tinge of embarrassment. "I have no clothes to wear to a ball." She opened her arms, and looked down at her filthy, torn clothing that was still slightly damp from the downpour she had created just a short while ago in her world. Even if they were clean, jeans were definitely not suitable attire for a fae ball. She knew Faen and Jocelyn could just magic themselves a wardrobe at the flick of a wrist.

"Do not worry, Faedra. I have a feeling the king would have thought of that," he gave her a warm smile.

Faedra's eyes widened with excitement. "See you later then," she said as ran into her room and made a beeline for the bed.

Faen raised his eyes heavenward and shook his head, a big smile curving his lips as he headed to his room.

"Oh wow, it's beautiful," Faedra gasped as she picked up the dress that had been laid out for her on the bed, and held it out in front of her.

It was made of luscious silk damask in the most beautiful color of green Faedra had ever seen. The pattern woven into the fabric shimmered as she moved it under the light. The dress was full length, the bodice was laced in the front and had a square neckline with a panel of gold silk running down the front to the floor. The bodice nipped in at the waist, and the dress fell from there into a full, flowing skirt that was heavily petticoated. The sleeves were long and wide, shaped into a point that hung down from the wrists. Faedra held it up to her and ran to the mirror. She admired the dress for a moment twisting from side to side, causing the skirt to rustle as it swung with her movement.

She returned the dress to the bed, making extra care to lay it out neatly so that it didn't wrinkle. She looked on the floor beside the bed to find a pair of silk slippers that matched the color of the dress to perfection and were trimmed with gold braid. Beside the dress was what Faedra thought at first glance, looked like a tiara, but when she picked it up to examine it, it was the wrong shape to fit on top of her head. She considered it carefully for a while, not quite sure where it should go.

It was beautiful, a band of delicate gold with a filigree pattern, which was open at the back and curved into a 'v' in the center from which a delicate gold pendant hung in a design that she recognized instantly. It was the same design as the center of Faen's talisman that hung around his neck.

She stared at it in awe for a moment, and then it occurred to her where she would wear it. This piece of jewelry was to be worn on her forehead. She replaced it carefully on the bed next to the dress.

Faedra peeled out of her dirty torn clothes, folded them up and laid them on the chair. She was not looking forward to having to put them back on in the morning. A bath was waiting for her just as before, and she soaked in its soothing hot water for a while before getting ready for the ball. She was astounded by what had been laid out for her. Beneath the mirror was an array of things she may need. There were clips and pins for her hair. The exact shades and types of makeup she used, and the brushes to apply them with.

"How do they know all this stuff?" she whispered to herself as she happily went about her usual routine of applying her makeup. She decided to pile her thick, curly red hair high on her head. Leaving the odd tendril to fall around her face and neck, which left her 'fairy' birthmark proudly on display. The dress and slippers fit her perfectly, she had no doubt that they would. She checked her appearance in the full-length mirror, and it surprised even her.

She chuckled at the corniness of it, she looked nothing short of a fairy princess.

"Finishing touch," she told herself as she picked up the piece of jewelry off the bed and walked over to the mirror. She slid it onto her forehead, the ends nestled securely in her hair, and it rested comfortably above her eyebrows.

There was a knock at the door.

"Come in," she called, and turned just as Faen entered.

He stopped dead upon seeing her, and she heard a definite catch in his breath. He had exactly the same affect on her. They stared at each other for a moment in silence.

He was wearing a cream shirt under an overcoat that was made of the same material as her dress. The sleeves of his overcoat were slit almost from the shoulder and fell behind his arms. The collarless front came down in a v and had one clasp holding it closed at the center. The overcoat came halfway down his thighs and the entire garment was edged with gold trim as were the cuff and collar of his shirt.

He smiled and it took her breath away. "You look beautiful," he said.

"Thank you. I have to admit I feel like a princess in this dress."

"It is not the dress that makes you a princess," he stated as he walked over to where Faedra was standing.

She gave him a questioning look, thinking that was an odd thing for him to say, but he didn't respond to her puzzled expression, so she thought no more of it.

When he reached her she looked up at him and pointed to the jewelry on her forehead. "This was you, not the king, wasn't it?"

"You do not mind do you?" he asked sheepishly.

"Mind?" she was surprised at his question. "No, why ever would I mind, Faen? It's beautiful."

He smiled. "I'm glad you like it."

"Is this design like some kind of family crest?"

"Yes, I believe you could call it that."

"Well then, I'm honored that you think highly enough of me to allow me to wear it," she said brimming with pride.

"Shall we?" he asked as he held out his arm for her to take. "Jocelyn is waiting for us in the corridor."

Faedra took his arm and they walked out of her room.

"Wow, Jocelyn you look fantastic," Faedra gasped as she caught sight of her friend. Jocelyn had traded her usual black and white dress for one that was a sumptuous purple velvet with a panel of shimmering lilac silk down the front. It also had a fitted bodice that laced at the front with a square neckline, and a full skirt that flowed to the floor, but her dress was sleeveless.

"Why thank you, Faedra, as do you."

They could hear the music playing as they approached the Great Hall. They got to the doors and were announced by a very austere looking fairy. The music stopped and people ceased their dancing to turn and look at them. Faedra could feel her cheeks heat up. Faen took hold of her hand and they continued into the hall. Everyone they passed either bowed or curtsied. Faedra wasn't quite sure how to react, so she kept nodding her head and smiling at everyone as they continued to where the king was sitting. When they got there the king clapped his hands twice and the music started again.

The Great Hall had been decorated extravagantly. Lots of silver and gold banners with the royal crest emblazoned upon them hung from the ceiling, and twinkling lights were wrapped around the columns. Faedra's attention turned to where the music was coming from. There was a group of musicians sitting to one side of the raised platform where the throne sat. A couple of older looking fairies with silver gray hair and neatly trimmed silver beards were playing mandolins. There was a younger fairy playing what looked like a flute, and a beautiful lady fairy playing a harp. The music they were creating was truly enchanting. She then turned her attention to the people dancing. There were lots of different kinds of people dancing, probably from other realms, too and they were doing a very good job of it. It was nothing like the dancing she had ever done. It involved at lot more movement, and looked much more complicated as they twirled and stepped and twirled again.

"May I have this dance?" Faen interrupted Faedra's thoughts.

"Oh, Err, Faen I can't dance like that," she said looking at the dancers swirling around with confidence and ease in front of them. Their timing and accuracy was something to behold. To be honest she'd rather take her chances with a sword and Vivianna than make a complete fool of herself in front of all these people and the king.

"Do you trust me?" he asked.

"That's a silly question, you know I do, with my life," she replied with a panicked look on her face. She knew where this was leading, straight onto the dance floor.

"Well in that case," he held his arm for her again.

"I'm not going to get out of this am I?" she said with a disgruntled look in her eyes.

He just smiled.

Faedra grimaced, and after taking a deep breath took his arm. She needn't have worried, as soon as they stepped onto the dance floor he made a movement with his head towards the musicians and they stopped the lively music they were playing, and started playing something soft and lilting. Everyone stopped dancing mid stride and paired up to continue dancing to the slower tune without even skipping a beat.

Faen led Faedra around the dance floor with so much confidence that she soon forgot her nerves, and could only focus on the face smiling down at her. She didn't even know how her feet were making their way round, nor did she care. The dance came to an end all too soon, and for a moment they stood in silence in the center looking at one another, completely oblivious of the people who were dancing around them.

"I need to show you something," Faen said after a long moment, his eyes shining with uncertainty.

"Okay," Faedra replied cautiously, wondering why he was looking uncertain. He very rarely looked uncertain.

Faen took hold of her hand and walked her out of the hall. Torches blazed along the walls of the corridor, lighting their way outside. The moon was out in all its silvery glory, shining its bright ethereal light onto the courtyard where they had stopped. They were bathed entirely in the moonlight now, out of reach of the golden glow from the torches in the castle. He turned Faedra to look at him, and took both of her hands in his. She noticed a slight tremble there and gave him a puzzled look.

"Close your eyes, please," he whispered.

She did as he asked.

"You may open them now," he said after only a heartbeat had passed.

She did as he asked again, and instantly sucked in a breath. Her jaw dropped, she couldn't find any words to describe what her eyes were seeing. She thought him beautiful before, but now with his wings proudly outstretched before her, it made her want to cry. She took a step back but didn't let go of his hands, and could feel tears of emotion pricking behind her eyes as she absorbed the picture of beauty standing right before her.

His wings were silvery white, at least that is how they looked in the moonlight. All around the edges they sparkled in gold, and an intricate golden design intertwined its way throughout his whole wingspan, which was twice the size of Jocelyn's although they were shaped similarly to his sister's. She had noticed that most of the fairies she had seen had wings of different shapes and sizes. She hadn't seen any that sparkled the way Faen's did right now though. Every inch of his wings glistened in the glow from the moon, and she could just imagine how much more vibrantly they must shimmer in the sunlight. Enchanting didn't even begin to describe them.

"Breathe, Faedra," Faen whispered after a moment.

Faedra brought her gaze to meet his. "Huh?" She was still speechless, it didn't happen very often. She pulled in a breath. "You're beautiful," she whispered.

"Thank you," he said softly with an incline of his head as he pulled her towards him.

She noticed his talisman hanging from his neck. "Your necklace, and my…" she touched the jewelry on her forehead, "it's the same design as your wings."

"Yes it is." He smiled at her observation.

"I don't think I'll ever get used to them you know," she whispered as she looked up at his wings again.

"Well you will have a very long time to try." He smiled again as he cupped her face in his hands.

She closed her eyes. His wings were emblazoned on the inside of her eyelids; they still sparkled there even when her eyes were shut.

As they kissed, Faedra was too distracted to pay any attention to the warm sensation traveling up her ring finger. Neither of them noticed the person lurking in the shadows who was glaring at them with such an icy stare it could have frozen fire, nor did they notice the tiny red laser lights that encircled her before she disappeared.

About the Author

Alison Pensy was born and raised in England. She grew up near a medieval city, which is where much of the inspiration for her books comes from. Moving to the States in 2001, she eventually settled near a small town in mid Missouri with her menagerie of animals.

Alison also runs her own tax and accounting business and started writing when she became so fed up with the real world, she decided to create her own.

Please visit her blog at www.alisonpensy.blogspot.com. She loves to hear from her readers, so feel free to leave comments or ask questions.

Made in the USA
Lexington, KY
10 June 2011